T0317963

Instructed to Play

An Erotica Collection

mischief

Mischief
An imprint of HarperCollins*Publishers*
77–85 Fulham Palace Road,
Hammersmith, London W6 8JB

www.mischiefbooks.com

A Paperback Original 2013

First published in Great Britain in ebook format by
HarperCollins*Publishers* 2012

A catalogue record for this book is
available from the British Library

ISBN-13: 9780007534838

Set in Sabon by FMG using Atomic ePublisher from Easypress

Find out more about HarperCollins and the environment at
www.harpercollins.co.uk/green

CONTENTS

Contents

Holding Still
Rose de Fer

The room hums with energy, as though the air is electrified. But within all is stillness. Silence and extraordinary stillness.

We are frozen, my sisters and I, maintaining the poses we have been instructed to hold while the potential buyers move among us, inspecting, assessing, admiring. I am lucky to have been given an easy position, probably because I'm the newest.

Across the gallery Helene balances on one leg, the other raised and bent slightly in front, as though she is about to step gracefully down from her pedestal. And next to her is Cerys, sitting with her legs stretched out along either side of a polished wooden beam. Both poses look extremely challenging and I'm envious of the balance it must take to maintain them.

My own pose is simple by comparison. I am kneeling naked, my head bowed, my eyes downcast. The very picture of submission. My hands rest by my sides, palms flat on the platform. My long hair has been coiled and pinned on top of my head so that the buyers can see my face. My expression is one of cultivated serenity, of deep contentment with my humble position.

Around me the men and women discuss the living statuary, asking questions of our curator and discussing prices. Two men and a woman enthuse over Natasha's display. She sits before a mirror, her long red hair swept over one shoulder. Like the girl in the Pre-Raphaelite painting she emulates, she is frozen in the act of combing her hair, a wistful expression on her face.

I listen to their comments as they discuss her price. A friendly argument ensues and one of the men finally names a figure that is too high for his companions. The sale is completed. Out of the corner of my eye I see Natasha rise from her stool and greet the man who is now her owner. They leave the room together and I feel a twinge of sadness knowing I won't see her again.

And then I feel the steady gaze of someone's eyes on me.

The spicy aroma of a man's cologne teases my nose as he circles me, quietly studying me. Voices waft across the room like currents of air but my observer is alone. Intrigued by what he sees, he reaches out a hand to caress my hip, my thigh. I remain perfectly still as I have been taught, willing away the gooseflesh that threatens to mar my smooth skin and spoil the illusion.

'Alina,' he says, reading my name off the little bronze plaque beneath me.

Seeing the man's interest in me, the curator approaches. He introduces himself and explains that I am new, that this is only my first exhibition, but that I have shown immense promise and he is sure I would be a worthy addition to any collector's home.

The man nods and reaches up to stroke my cheek. He traces a finger down my throat and along the curve of one bare breast. He cups me gently and I feel my nipple stiffen in response to his touch. It's exactly the kind of reaction collectors want, the kind that surprises one into remembering that we are human after all. He laughs softly.

'She's very responsive.' He slides his thumb over the hard little bud, sending a jolt of pleasure through my body. I focus all my concentration on maintaining my position. I must not sigh or gasp or moan. I mustn't close my eyes or even flutter an eyelash. I am a statue. One of warm flesh and blood rather than alabaster but a statue nonetheless.

The man draws his hand down along my pale arm to my wrist. Then he presses against the delicate skin to feel my pulse. Doubtless my heart is beating faster now than when he first approached me and his touch makes it beat even faster. He gives another appreciative laugh.

'Yes, very responsive.'

He has a nice voice, cultured and kind. I like the warmth in his touch, the amusement in his tone as he examines the rest of me, stroking the soles of my upturned feet and running a finger down the line of my spine. My legs are closed but he comments favourably on my smoothly shaved mound. I fight the blush that threatens to stain my cheeks as he asks whether he might part my thighs to see the rest.

The curator agrees and my admirer gently eases my legs apart. My knees slide easily against the polished surface on which I'm kneeling and soon I feel the caress of cool air against my nether lips. I try to slow my breathing, willing my racing heart to be calm. But when the man draws his fingers up along my inner thigh and sweeps them gently across the slick folds of my sex I feel my pulse jump again. It's all I can do to keep from closing my eyes at the stimulation.

'Very nice indeed,' he says. He steps back and looks me over once again. For several moments I feel as though I am suspended over a vast chasm as I wait to hear his verdict. After what seems an eternity, he ends the torment. 'Yes. I think she would be a lovely addition to my collection.'

My sex throbs in response but it's a reaction no one

can see. Neither can they see the way I clench the inner muscles to send another little spasm of pleasure through my body. My mind whirls as I try to imagine what my new owner will do with me, how he will display me. I've heard of girls made to act as the centrepiece at a lavish feast, others to liven up a garden or the foyer of a grand house. For some reason I have always pictured myself displayed in an alcove, perhaps at the top of a curving staircase. Of course, it's not up to me to choose.

The curator stands before me and places a fatherly hand on my shoulder. 'Alina, it's time to go. Mr Villiers will take you home now.'

It's always difficult to move after holding still for so long. After a while the stillness becomes second nature and I forget I'm able to move at all. I raise my head slowly and meet the eyes of my new master. A smile plays at the corners of his lips and I return it, blushing. He puts his arm around me, helps me up and leads me away.

* * *

My new home is a sprawling Victorian estate set far back from the main road. A maid opens the door for Mr Villiers but she didn't bat an eye at me. But for the velvet cloak he fastened around me to keep me warm, I am still naked.

He leads me through the house to a vast and elegant library. Ornate bookshelves climb the walls to the high ceiling and a fire crackles warmly in the massive hearth. The furniture has clearly been arranged with the display of a statue in mind. Two plush sofas and a scattering of chairs all face in towards a round marble plinth about two feet high and topped with a red silk cushion. Mr Villiers removes my cloak and lays it over the arm of a chair. Then he lifts me easily and places me on top of the plinth.

Now comes the moment I have always dreamed of. My master tells me to demonstrate a series of poses for him so that he may choose the one he likes best. Of course, statues need not stay the same; part of the appeal in a living statue is her variety. Rather than buy a new piece of art one can simply instruct the statue to adopt a new pose.

I show him all the poses I have been taught, some of which make me feel both dread and hope that he'll choose them because of the challenge they would offer me. I want to please him. He nods his head at each and gestures for me to show him the next one. I'm nearing the end of my repertoire but he still hasn't picked one.

'Hmm,' he says, frowning thoughtfully. 'I did rather like the way you were displayed at the gallery.'

I immediately sink to my knees and drop my head, arranging myself in the submissive posture he first saw

6

me in. He eyes me critically for a moment before shaking his head.

'It's still not quite right.'

He begins to position me himself. He parts my legs as he did before and I feel myself grow damp with the exposure. With a gentle hand on my bottom he urges me up off my heels a few inches so that my thighs take my weight. Then he places my arms behind my back, my wrists crossed as if bound. Finally, he presses against my back, encouraging me to arch my spine. The position forces my small breasts forwards and I blush deeply at the powerful feeling of submission the pose evokes in me. He adjusts my head by tilting my chin up until my head is level with his chest. I gaze at the pattern of his tie, a passionate design of red and black swirls.

'Eyes down,' he tells me.

I obey.

He nods his approval and steps away. I hear his retreating footsteps and then the opening of a drawer from somewhere behind me. When he returns to me I see he has the little bronze plaque from the gallery, the one with my name on it. He fixes it into its setting at the base of the plinth and I am still. From this moment on I am his statue. An object he has purchased to decorate his beautiful library. I must hold this pose with absolute stillness until I am released.

Warmth courses through my body at the thought of

the lovely pose he has created for me and I focus all my energy on maintaining it. It's not as easy as it looks. My thighs are working the hardest, opened wide and angled forty-five degrees up and away from the plinth, supporting my weight. After a while I know they will be aching and possibly even trembling with the effort. But it wouldn't be considered an art if it were easy or comfortable. And it wouldn't be so erotic if it weren't such a challenge.

Mr Villiers moves around the room, observing me from different angles and commenting favourably on what he sees. The maid returns when summoned and I am not surprised to learn from his conversation with her that guests will shortly be arriving. I wait until he has left the room for a moment to make a minute adjustment to my position. I won't get another chance once the room is full of people scrutinising me. The thought warms me inside and I recall the silky touch of his finger between my legs at the gallery. I replay the moment again and again in my mind as I listen to the voices of the men and women entering the room and seeing their friend's new acquisition.

'How lovely!' a lady exclaims. There is a flash of colour to my left as she comes closer and then she strokes the hollow of my hip with cool fingers.

A man beside her touches me in a similar fashion. Then another. Then another. The sensation of so many hands on me is powerfully erotic but I remember my training and keep my breathing slow and steady. I can't help the gallop of my heart but I focus on being still, being obedient.

'Isn't she exquisite?' someone says.

'I must get one like her for my study.'

'Perhaps I can find a matching pair for the garden.'

All around me words of praise float in the air and admiring hands roam over me as they might any decorative object. A lady draws her lacquered red nails down over my thighs. A man pinches my toes. Another tickles the tender crease between buttock and thigh. But I frustrate their attempts to make me react.

'I do feel rather like Pygmalion.'

My master's voice cuts through the chattering of the others and I time my breathing so that my next slow exhalation comes only after he has touched me again. I would recognise his touch even with all my other senses blocked, but I can smell his cologne and the musky warmth of his skin as he stands beside me. His fingertips tease my jutting pelvic bone as he slides his hand around to caress my bottom. The others fall silent while he strokes his possession. His touch is the hardest to resist responding to.

After a while a lady speaks. 'But your Galatea hasn't come to life yet.'

This is both the central irony and central beauty of my art, that I am most alive when pretending to be made of stone.

'Oh, but I think she has,' my master says. His hand slides up along the arch of my spine and then around to my left side. He gives my breast a little squeeze before pressing his hand up underneath it, hard against my ribs. I can feel my heart beating against his fingers, as though it's trying to reach him. Heat floods my face and radiates through the rest of me, finding a home in the silky wet folds of my sex.

As though he can smell my arousal he laughs softly and then his hand is between my legs. 'Very alive indeed,' he murmurs.

And he's right. I am more alive than I have ever been. More alive than at any other time in my life. My sex pulses feverishly in time with my pounding heart as his fingers probe and explore the soft wetness. And when he slips a finger deep inside me I can't help it – I gasp. It's only a tiny sound but it may as well be the shattering of glass. The shattering of an illusion.

I freeze again immediately but the damage is done. And now I can't help the trembling in my legs as my master frowns.

'Oh, dear,' he says, and his disappointment is agony for me.

I daren't speak, not even to apologise. The best I can hope for is that he'll excuse my lapse. The curator explained that I was new, after all.

A man's laugh rings out in the silent room, as jarring as a horn. 'Well, it looks like your Galatea has a voice!'

The others laugh at that and one by one they slip away to the dining room. Someone calls out to my master, to ask if he is coming. But he shakes his head, standing before me as still as a statue himself.

'It would seem,' he says calmly, 'that you are not yet fully trained after all.'

My trembling intensifies and I feel tears pricking my eyes. My very first private exhibition and I have failed. The shame threatens to overwhelm me.

'But no matter. What's done is done. We're none of us perfect, are we?'

I know better than to deepen my disgrace by responding as though he had asked the question of a person. Flawed or not, I am still a statue and must hold on to as much of my role as I can.

'No,' he continues, his voice kind and forgiving. I sense his smile as he smoothes a strand of hair behind my ear. 'Not perfect. Which means I have the pleasure of teaching you how to mimic perfection.'

My heart seems to stumble in my chest as I realise he isn't going to send me back. Immediately I regain control of myself, will my eyes to stop welling with tears, will my body to stop shaking. I focus on the red and black swirls in his tie and lose myself in the pattern as I try to disengage from my body. I think of Natasha and the other girls, so silent and still, so perfect. How can I ever hope to be as good as they are?

'You will have to earn your submissive pose again,' he says. Then he paces away across the room and when he returns he is holding a riding crop.

If my eyes widen slightly he doesn't notice, as he is inspecting the looped leather tongue at the end of the crop. He slaps it against his palm a few times. Then he slices the crop through the air before me and I can't help it: I flinch.

He tuts and shakes his head. 'Statues do not react,' he says, and his tone is inscrutable. 'Not to noises or touches. Not to pleasure or pain. Not to any stimuli at all.'

I still the trembling that threatens to overwhelm me and he holds the crop out, pressing the tongue firmly against my left nipple. The leather is cool and I immediately stiffen beneath its touch. He does the same on the other side and I suppress a shiver. My focus is completely gone and I can't seem to regain it. Quite apart from my horror at having failed him, I'm both frightened and aroused by his authority. I desperately want to please him, to earn my pose back and to be touched again like before.

He raises the crop a few inches and then flicks it down onto the hard peak of my nipple. Not enough to hurt, just enough to send a flash of stimulation through me. It's all I can do not to react but I hold myself still for him as he moves to the other side and repeats the stroke. He watches my face closely as he positions the crop again and taps me gently. This time he brings it down with a little more force.

The sensation is intense on such a delicate part of me and I can't fully process what I'm feeling. The smack of leather is impossible to ignore. It awakens all the sensitive nerve endings, sending a confusing blend of signals through me. Pleasure, pain and something in between.

He moves the crop back and forth, bringing it down in a brisk motion on first one nipple, then the other. A little harder each time now. I force myself to stay still, to resist the urge to cry out, gasp or whimper. When I realise I'm not breathing I make myself inhale slowly and hold the breath for several seconds before letting it out just as slowly.

The crop descends smartly, again and again, daring me to defy the man inflicting the torment. But I breathe through the strokes, determined to pass his test, determined to make him proud of me. My nipples tingle from the strange stimulation and the burning flows through my body like waves until my sex is throbbing in response.

When he finally stops I feel strangely bereft. Then my master tucks the crop under his arm to free both his hands. He cups my aching breasts, and the warmth of his palms against the burning skin of my nipples is both soothing and agonising. Even then, I don't allow myself to react. He'll be able to feel the wild pounding of my heart but I hope I have borne the punishment to his satisfaction.

'Very good,' he says.

Before I can relax, however, he takes up the crop again and this time places the leather tongue up against my sex. Tingling with fear and excitement, I brace myself.

The first stroke is gentle, just a little tap. But my sex is even more sensitive than my breasts and the smack of leather is like a jolt of electricity. The next stroke is harder and the next is harder still. I feel each one deep inside me, penetrating me as his finger did earlier.

Although I hold perfectly still for him, there is no doubt that he can see how much his actions are arousing me. Each smack of the crop against my wetness floods me with sensation and when he flicks the tip back and forth across my clit I realise with sudden alarm that he intends to make me come. My eyes must reflect some fear over this because he gives a low chuckle and the crop ceases its relentless assault for a moment. My sex tingles along with my breasts, burning and pulsing at the sensory onslaught, wanting more.

But he teases me. He steps around to my side and now he rests the crop against the smooth curve of my bottom. I hold my breath as I feel it lift away and then connect with a sharp smack. He is less forgiving here, laying on the strokes smartly and giving me less time to recover in between. It's all I can do not to yelp and flinch.

Then the leather tongue, warmer now that it has tasted so much of my tender flesh, taps against the delicate soles of my feet. I wait, every muscle tensed in anticipation, until he raises the crop again and it strikes in earnest. The pain is astonishing. But it's also exhilarating. As it rises and falls against my feet I feel a surge of euphoria. I have crossed a line where pain becomes pleasure and all sensation is welcome.

As though sensing the change in me, my master returns to stand in front of me. He caresses my face, cups my chin and slips his thumb into my mouth, teasing my tongue with it like the promise of a kiss. Through it all I remain perfectly still although every nerve in my body is screaming for release.

He steps back and presses the end of the crop between my legs again. My nether lips are burning and swollen from the punishment they have taken but they still want more. I want more.

He doesn't make me wait long. I feel the crop tap gently against my inner thighs, peppering them with light little smacks before returning for a more vigorous assault on my sex. The leather strikes me hard, harder, harder, and the wave begins to build inside me. He adjusts the angle just enough to catch my clit and each sharp stroke drives me closer and closer. When the rush overtakes me I lose all sense of control, crying out with complete abandon as a pleasure more intense than I ever thought possible threatens to consume me.

He catches me before I can fall and my body assaults me from within as I gasp and pant and tremble in his arms.

After a while he releases me and it takes some effort to stand upright after what I've just endured. I blush fiercely as he forces me to meet his eyes. He is smiling.

'Hello, Galatea,' he says.

I try to return his smile but, although I'm buzzing with pleasure at what he's done to me, I still can't help but feel terrible for my earlier failure. 'I'm sorry,' I murmur, not sure what else to say.

His laugh surprises me. 'The whole point of having a statue is so that you can bring her to life.'

He lifts me up and sets me back on my plinth. I sink to my knees and he arranges me in my pose, my knees apart, back arched, eyes down.

'Now,' he says, 'you have both earned your submission and been rewarded. I'm going to call my guests back in and this time I expect my little statue to remain a statue. For them anyway. I'm sure she's learned now the proper time to awaken.'

I have. I nod my understanding meekly. It's the last time I will move until we're alone again.

I'm tingling in all the places where the crop has kissed me and I imagine my skin is red and marked from the little leather tongue. It will be no secret to the others what has happened, what's been done to me. I also imagine I now radiate a glow of ecstasy, an invitation, a challenge. Let them try and distract me, to make me react. I will come to life again, but only my master will see it.

Penance for the Perverse
Heather Towne

Joe and Mary fell in love almost as soon as Mary arrived in Joe's small hometown. She had lived in a large city on the west coast, and was now seeking a simpler, more spiritual life in the rolling hills of northern Idaho. Joe was thirty-two and lonely, a respected teacher at the local elementary school and parishioner in the Pine Hills Baptist Church. Mary was thirty-five and longing for a good man and a good life. They were married in Joe's church two months after first meeting.

Mary was a lapsed Catholic. Now, she embraced Joe's religion, born-again into Christianity. Joe couldn't believe how lucky he was to have found such a loving, beautiful wife to share his faith and life with, raise a family. He was a tall man, with thinning black hair and a pale, chiselled face, bright-blue eyes and full red lips, a wiry physique. Mary was petite, pretty, with wavy chestnut-brown hair and large violet eyes, an oval face and plush pincushion lips, large breasts and ample buttocks, tawny skin.

It was a month after their nuptials, as they sat in front of the fireplace after Sunday dinner, that Mary said to her husband, 'Joe, I have a confession to make.' She looked down at her delicate hands in her lap, her voluptuous body clad in a simple black dress.

Joe glanced up from the textbook he'd been studying. He smiled, his handsome face beaming contentedly. 'Confession? Why, what do you mean, Mary?'

Mary sighed. 'Well, in my old church, we used to confess our sins every Sunday – to, well, cleanse our souls, so to speak. Confess any sinful things we'd done or any sinful thoughts we'd had during the week. Then take penance for it. But in your – I mean, our – church, there's no such thing as a confessional.' She licked her lips, batted her long, dark eyelashes at her husband. 'So, I'd like to confess something to you, Joe, have you punish me with any penance you see fit.'

Joe set the textbook aside and patted his lap. 'I doubt if I could ever punish you, Mary.'

Mary rose and walked over to him, sat down in her husband's lap. Her lush buttocks spread warm and soft against the crotch of his Sunday suit pants, her shapely legs dangling over his. She coiled an arm around his neck, and he gripped her waist.

'Go ahead, dear,' Joe said. 'If you want to.'

Mary nodded, gazing into her husband's loving eyes. 'Well, when Reverend Okoye was giving his sermon this morning ...'

Joe squeezed his wife's waist and placed a warm, gentle hand on her left thigh, smiling beatifically up at her.

'... I imagined myself sucking his cock,' Mary stated.

Joe's hands froze on his wife's body. He stared at her.

'He's such a fine-looking man, you know. I realise he's married, like we are, but I just couldn't help thinking about going down on my knees in front of him, as he gave his sermon, and pulling his long hard black cock out of his vestments and swirling my tongue all around his bulbous purple hood, teasing some pre-come out of his gaping slit and slurping it up. Then painting his pipe with my tongue, licking all up and down his swollen shaft, making it shine and throb. Before sliding my lips right over his cockhead and down his shaft, consuming his prick right to the blue-black balls. Then gripping his hips and bobbing my head back and forth, sucking tight and wet and deep on his huge, heavy dong.'

Mary's fingers bit into Joe's neck, and she squirmed in his lap, her eyes shining and lips moist, breath bathing her husband's shocked face in warm, humid air. He gaped at her, sitting rigid, hands clutching her waist and leg.

19

Mary went on, 'I sucked his cock for a good long time – up on the stage, with the whole congregation watching – until I tasted more hot, salty pre-come, leaking down my throat. Then I pulled his cock out of my mouth and hooked my finger and thumb around the dripping shaft, just below the swelled hood, cutting off his flow of semen. I pushed his prick up and my head down and kissed his big, hanging balls, licked at his sac, batted his nuts around with my tongue. He just grunted and went on with his sermon, so I swallowed his entire pouch in my mouth and pulled on it, looking up at him from around his pulsating ebony dong.'

Joe gulped, croaked, 'You–you were thinking all this ... when ...'

Mary smiled and kissed her husband on his trembling lips, rubbing her butt cheeks against the hardening length of cock she could feel under her bum. Her pussy was warm and sticky with moisture, her nipples thick and buzzing against her dress.

'I know it's wrong, honey. That's why I'm telling you. While I was sucking on the minister's balls, pumping his cock with my hand, all the parishioners were staring at me, watching me commit oral sex on the reverend. But no one tried to stop me; they were all as turned-on as I was. I teabagged Reverend Okoye for a long time, thoroughly sucking his sac, breathing deep of his musky, masculine scent. Even with his balls bulging my mouth,

I slid my tongue out and licked at his perineum. That's when he spasmed and pulled back, forcing me to spit out his nuts. He lifted me up to my feet and led me over to the altar table, his jutting cock and hung balls shining with my saliva. I was already totally naked, so he just laid me out on my back on the table and gripped his gleaming staff and –'

'Mary! That's enough! How–how could you?'

Mary nodded, her eyes sparkling. 'I know. It's sinful, isn't it, Joe? That's why I had to tell you. That's why I need penance – have to be punished by you, my husband.'

She undulated her bum against Joe's stiffened cock some more, then swung out of his tented lap, draped herself over his shaking knees. She pulled the skirt of her conservative dress up, exposing her big bare bottom. She shuddered the twin caramel mounds of her buoyant butt cheeks, looking up at her husband. 'Whatever punishment you think is appropriate, Joe.'

He stared down at his wife's humped, boisterous bottom, his face and body burning with heat. He tore his right hand off the armrest of the chair and lifted it into the air.

Mary quivered, her body shimmering with anticipation. 'Reverend Okoye plunged his cockhead into my pussy, ploughed his shaft into my tunnel. Oh, Joe, I was so full of his cock that my head spun, my cunt stretched like it's never been –'

Crack! Joe struck his wife's ass with his hand.

She jumped, gasped. Her soft, sensitive back-mounds shivered wickedly, the imprint of her husband's bladed hand flaming red on the honey-coloured flesh for a moment.

'He pulled my legs up to his chest, his dong buried inside of me. But he kept right on sermonising, Joe, as he pumped his hips, churning his cock back and forth in my pussy. The congregation watched and listened with rapt attention. I grasped my splayed breasts and squeezed and –'

Crack! Joe slammed his hand down onto Mary's bum a second time. She jumped again, gasped again, her breasts and buttocks and body rippling.

'And I pushed my tits right up to my mouth and sucked on my own nipples, getting banged back and forth on the altar table by the pumping force of Reverend Okoye's cock. He was so big and powerful –'

Crack! Crack! Crack!

Joe flat-out spanked his wife, smashing his hand down on her buttocks again and again and again. His body shivered with the force of the blows like hers did, Mary's butt cheeks burning red under his whaling hand, gyrating wildly as his and her feelings.

'He kept fucking and fucking me, pounding into my pussy. I knew he wouldn't come until the end of his sermon, he had so much stamina. But I was sure I couldn't hold out, his sawing pleasure sending me sailing.'

Joe's hand whistled up and down, striking fast and furious, the crack of hardened flesh against soft skin sounding loud and clear and lewd in the hushed, homey living room. Mary could feel her husband's cock beating against her belly, as he beat her bottom. She surged joyously with each smashing blow, her pussy staining Joe's pants with hot, leaking juices.

'I could hardly bear it, Joe! He was reaming my pussy, stretching and stuffing me. I rolled my head around on the table, kneading my tits, pulling on my nipples, the joy building and building inside of me, his cock pumping me full of wild passion. Until ...'

Joe slammed his wife's ass over and over, lifting and crashing faster and faster, brutally hard. His arm ached and his palm burned, his face flaming hot as Mary's bum cheeks, his cock surging against her rocking body. He had to punish her. She needed it, demanded it, deserved it. He thrilled with it, like her.

The living room was filled with the vicious cracking of Joe's hand on Mary's ass, Joe's laboured breathing, Mary's gasps and groans. The frenzy built to towering heights, sweat pouring down Joe's face. Mary's bum throbbed, almost brick-red under the onslaught.

Joe whacked Mary's blazing bottom one final time, then bucked up against her. She felt his warm, wet spurts against her stomach, his spasming cock spouting out orgasm. She reached up and grabbed on to his spank-hot hand and jammed it down sideways in between her legs, pumped his rigid fingers against her sopping wet pussy.

'He exploded inside of me, blasting me with burst after burst of fiery heat as he concluded his sermon! Finally allowing me blessed release!' Mary jerked, orgasm erupting in her pussy alongside Joe's scrubbing fingers and storming through her body in superheated waves. 'And all the male parishioners got up and swarmed all around me and jerked off over my writhing body, coating my face and tits in their sticky rapture!'

Mary's head flopped down, and her body went limp over her husband's quivering knees. He stared blankly down at her battered bottom, his fingers still pressed up against her simmering pussy, his crotch drenched with semen.

Joe and Mary murmured, 'Amen!' together.

* * *

Mary's next confession came less than a week later, after she and Joe had attended a wedding at their church. Joe was making a fire in the living-room fireplace of their rustic bungalow on the wooded edge of their small town, while Mary sat in her chair knitting.

'Karen looked beautiful in her wedding dress, didn't she, Joe?' Mary commented.

Joe lit a kitchen match, applied the flame to shredded

newspaper at the base of the three logs he'd stacked up. 'Yes,' he responded, 'she did.' He turned his head and gazed at his wife. 'But you looked even more –'

'I have a confession to make, Joe,' Mary stated, setting her knitting down.

The wooden match fell out of Joe's suddenly stiffened fingers, sparking a small blaze on the carpet that he quickly stomped out. He stared at his wife.

She smiled, sitting upright in her chair in the long-skirted blue dress she'd worn to the wedding. Her auburn hair was still done up, coils dangling down, her pretty face dusted with make-up, lips glistening red. Joe was still wearing his good white shirt and striped tie, his black suit pants, the shine on his black dress shoes reflecting the growing flames in the fireplace.

'Mary, I don't know if –'

'I imagined I was up there with Karen and her lovely bridesmaids, and Karen and I were kissing, as everybody watched. Her tongue darted into my mouth, wet and eager, and we swirled our tongues together, right in front of the minister. I ran my fingers through her long, silky blonde hair, and she ran her hands down my back and onto my bum cheeks, our tongues dancing out in the open for all to see. Then I painted her soft wet lips with my tongue, then bit into her long silken neck, our large breasts squishing together, she in her white lace wedding dress and me in a body-hugging black tuxedo.'

Joe swallowed, hard. He barely felt the heat from the crackling fire; it was the heat of his wife's words that was making him burn. There was a growing bulge in between his legs, swelling out the front of his pants.

'We sucked on each other's tongues for a moment, and then I pushed Karen's wedding dress right off her buff shoulders, and it fell down to her waist, exposing her round breasts. I cupped her creamy-white tits, feeling their warmth and weight, revelling in their smoothness. Then I kissed my way down Karen's chest to her breasts, licked in between them. The bridesmaids gathered around us, Lindsay, Alisha and Amy. I felt their hands on my back and my butt, caressing me, their fingers running through my hair. But I kept on squeezing Karen's breasts, licking all over the swollen mounds, twirling my tongue right around her engorging nipples, stretching them up higher and harder with my tongue.'

Joe reached down and gripped the poker, lifted it. But then he looked down at the lethal iron instrument, and dropped it. There was a yardstick leaning against the side of his chair. He'd brought it home from school for some sketches he was making of a possible addition to their house – a nursery. He walked over, picked up the three-foot-long wooden ruler and lightly smacked it against the palm of his left hand. His erection tented out his pants.

'I sucked on Karen's breasts, clutching them up and

nursing on them, taking the stiff, rubbery tips into my mouth and pulling on them with my lips, bobbing my head back and forth between her luscious breasts and succulent nipples. Karen grabbed on to my head, moaning, arching her chest into my mouth. Until I kissed and licked my way down to her stomach, leaving her nipples all shiny, her breasts heaving up and down. I pulled her wedding dress with me as I went down, so that when I reached her bellybutton, squirmed the tip of my tongue inside, her dress had dropped right down to her feet, and her beautiful blonde pussy was right in front of me. She was as wet as I was, Joe.'

Mary stood up and shed her own dress, stepped out of it and walked over to her husband in her sensible black heels, her body starkly naked. Her breasts shuddered and her buttocks swished, hips swaying, her pussy winking with moisture. Joe took her hand and positioned her in front of the fireplace. She gripped the stone mantle and spread her legs back, pushed her butt out, the orange flames making her heated body glow.

'I slid my hands down onto her bum and dug my fingernails into the thick, round flesh, dug my tongue in between Karen's long legs and licked her juicy pussy.'

Joe loosened his pants and shoved them down over his cock. He stood to the side, yardstick and cock raised, both wooden instruments twitching, straining to be used.

'She was so wet and tangy. I dragged my tongue over

her pussy again and again, her fur and her lips, lapping at the woman's cunt.'

Whack! The long hard ruler cracked across Mary's buttocks.

She jumped, fingernails scraping stone. She arched her back and her bum. 'I stuck my tongue right inside her, Joe, eating out her hot pussy. I shot my hands up onto her breasts and squeezed them some more, rolling her nipples, as I writhed my tongue around inside her velvety pink tunnel.'

Whack! Whack! Whack!

Joe's cock jumped along with Mary's body, pearls of pre-come flipping out of his slit, as he slashed her bottom with the yardstick. Both husband and wife burned in the heat of the fire, of their passion, white streaks flashing across Mary's buttocks where the ruler struck, then smouldering red, striping her brazen brown bottom.

'But just before Karen came in my mouth, on the end of my tongue, her bridesmaids lifted me up and stretched me out on the altar table. They were all as naked as Karen and I. They fondled me, kissed me, their hands all over me – then their mouths. Alisha and Lindsay sucked on my breasts, while Amy sucked on my tongue. And then Karen climbed up onto the table with me. She straddled my head with her knees, looking down at me from over her tits in her hands, her wedding veil still on. She stuck her sodden cunt right in my face and I grabbed on to her bum and licked as hard as I could. Lindsay and Alisha gripped and squeezed my tits and sucked on my jutting nipples, Amy now licking the length of my brimming slit.'

Joe slammed the ruler against his wife's ass in a frenzy, flailing her butt with the only slightly flexible wood. Mary rocked forward, almost right into the fire, her thrust-back, blazing buttocks gyrating wildly.

Joe gasped for air, his arm sore, his cock throbbing. But still he blasted blow after blow into Mary's bottom, welting her cheeks with ridges. Until, suddenly, the yard-stick snapped across his wife's shuddering butt, breaking in two.

'Oh, Joe!' Mary cried, sticking her blistered bum even further out and up, begging for more. 'Things got even wilder, more depraved. Because, suddenly, Amy and Alisha were wearing strap-ons – long black dildos strapped to their hips and bottoms, just like men's cocks, only bigger. And I was on top of Amy up on the altar table, stretched out on my back on top of her hot tits and body, Alisha kneeling in between my spread legs. Amy played the bloated tip of her dildo around my bum pucker, while Alisha dragged her cockhead over my pussy lips. They were going to double-penetrate me, Joe, as I sucked on Karen's pussy.'

Joe threw the splintered foot and a half of yardstick away, desperately looked around the living room.

'Your belt, Joe!' his wife urged. 'Use your belt!'

Joe dived down and ripped the wide black leather belt out of the loops of his fallen pants, rose back up. He gripped the buckle, folded the leather length back once, then raised the tanning instrument, glaring at Mary's brazen ass, his cock straining.

'Amy plunged her dong into my ass, and Alisha speared hers into my pussy. I almost burst with feeling, with passion – a huge black dildo stuffing my bum, another one stuffing my pussy. I slurped wildly on Karen's slit, Amy pumping my chute, Alisha my cunt.'

Joe cracked the belt across Mary's buttocks, whipping the woman. She shrieked, jolted shuddering onto her toes, her bum cheeks seared with the white stripe laid down by the black leather. Joe slashed her again, and again, and again, the belt streaking through the air, striking Mary's bottom with flailing impact, shattering husband and wife.

'Amy fucked me up the ass, Alisha fucked my pussy, the girls pumped full-length into my burning holes with their tremendous dongs. Meanwhile Lindsay sucked on my nipples and squeezed my boobs. And I hung onto Karen's rippling bum cheeks and lapped her dripping cunt like a madwoman. I could hardly comprehend what was happening, what I was feeling, my emotions so wickedly wanton.'

Joe lashed Mary with his belt, blasting red and white

stripes all over her ass, raising welts of stung, steaming flesh and then crushing them flat again. He was covered in sweat, gasping for breath, his cock jumping with every flogging blow, pre-come still flinging out of his slit. It went on and on and on, Mary's fingernails breaking on the stone mantle, body bouncing brutally to the savage song of the improvised whip.

Until, finally, Joe threw the heated belt aside and crowded right in behind his quivering wife. He plunged his cock into her molten pussy.

Mary moaned, gasped, 'Everybody in the church was watching us. Karen screamed, pulling on her nipples, her bum cheeks quivering in my hands, her pussy drenching my face. I lapped her slit, drinking in all I could, giving the gushing bride the best wedding gift of all. And then I was gifted with joy, too.'

Joe grabbed on to Mary's breasts, slamming his cock back and forth in her pussy. He thumped against his wife's blistered buttocks, pounding in the pleasure pussy and bum, plumbing the depths of both their sexualities with his cock.

'Amy and Alisha frantically plugged my anus and pussy, Lindsay biting into my nipples, almost tearing them off. I was sent heavenward. Oh, Joe! I came so hard and so –'

She spasmed, jumping in her husband's arms, on the end of his wildly churning cock. He jerked with his own searing orgasm, jetting inside her. The pair shuddered and squirted in front of the roaring blaze, joined in holy brimstone ecstasy of pussy and cock.

* * *

As a born-again Christian, Mary was only too glad to confess her sins. As a former adult actress with over 200 pornos under her belt, she had committed many such sins. Getting fucked by a minister in front of his flock with a follow-up group facial; lezzing it up with a bride and her bridesmaids in front of their wedding guests; these were but two of the scorching scenarios she had participated in on film.

She had only to wait for her bum to partially heal, before she'd 'confess' more such 'fantasies' to her righteously loving husband. So he could dish out her penance of perverse punishment, the pleasure of which they would both share in.

Transformation
Poppy St Vincent

She looked at herself in the steamy bathroom mirror. Naked, she screwed up her eyes and surveyed the image. Turning left and right she looked at her tummy and her bottom and sighed. She saw curves everywhere.

'Can that ever be a good thing?' she wondered out loud.

Turning her face to the left and the right she pinned her hair up, trying to see beyond her own perceptions, how another would see her.

The bath was hot. She eased slowly in, the heat reminding her of *ofuro*, the Japanese baths of a lifetime ago. Indeed she sat for some minutes with the gentle formality of a Japanese lady before she gave up and eased back and down into the water.

The water was soft pink and petals rested on the smooth surface. She skimmed a finger to push the petals, to form a queue, she thought. She wanted to see order in the chaos. Breathing in the scent of jasmine and clary sage she allowed herself to relax and reflect.

* * *

The day started out so well. The scent of autumn cutting through the frayed ends of summer met her as she left the house for work. She wore a scarf and a light jumper, a combination that pleased her. It reminded her of child-hood walks and crunchy leaves, of firelight, laughter and burnished reds and golds. She was doused in optimism until she looked in her post box and read the printing on the outside of a letter. A slow nausea crept over her as she slipped a finger along the crease and opened the envelope.

It was a fine notice – a fine of hundreds of pounds for not renewing her car tax, which she had had the money to pay but had not. What made her flood with guilt was that she had sworn to him, with wide and believable eyes, that she had paid it. She had even persuaded herself that she had done so. It had just been one of those dull little jobs that she did not want to do; spending money on a stupid piece of paper seemed such a waste. She had ignored it at first and then lied to make herself seem more efficient and then, when she remembered it in the dead of night, she just hoped somehow that she could ignore it and be let off.

When she was a child her father used to lend her money all the time and not once had she to repay it. It seemed so unfair to have to learn now that the world was not her benevolent father. Therein lay the problem, and it had led to this horrid, officious, formal telling-off, with barbs on.

She knew the issue would not be the money. If she needed that amount for something there would be no problem. The problem was the needless expense and the twenty-something different lies she had told to cover it up. Just moments before, she had felt so good, so on top of it all, but the letter made her feel fed up and useless. She felt stupid and that was so much worse than being in trouble.

All day she kept up the rhetoric of petty recrimination. The sustained and personal attack left her sad and strained by the end of the day and so when her beloved rang to suggest dinner she felt humbled by his offer and his ability to love such a fool and a failure.

She drove home and allowed a plan to gather, like birds flocking on telephone wires to await the flight from winter. She had made a mistake, she reasoned, and more than that she had chosen to lie, which was a blow to their relationship and was disapproved of by both of them. Except that his disapproval led to her being upended over his lap and dealt with in ways that made sitting a horrid experience and embarrassed her for days after. She simply would not tell him what had happened.

Her reasons were simple, considerate and mostly about him. He would be tired after a long day and would not wish to have another problem to deal with. A loving girlfriend meets her beloved with cheerful countenance. She had beaten herself up all day in ways that he would never dream of and so had paid for all her wrongdoing. She felt rubbish and unhappy and he wanted her to be happy, so that was what she should be.

She lay in the bath trying to reconcile her self-recrimination with an intention of feeling good and confident and in control.

The water had gone tepid while she was lost in her reverie, and she shook herself and then smoothed soap over her buffed skin to bring a delicate scent to every pore, disguising the turmoil just beneath the surface. She needed to reinvent herself, for him, for both of them.

The theatre of lotions and potions, their scent and the motion of application convinced her that it was possible to transform herself from total stuff-up and useless failure to fabulous lady, with only lotions and potions and creams and some terribly expensive underwear for her tools.

Towel-dried, she picked up her most treasured body

lotion (price, a girl secret) and as she slicked it all over she did indeed feel different. She breathed in a scent of grown-up confidence. Her legs were so smooth that the stockings glided up them as if they knew their place, the seams taking only moments to straighten as she did her Betty Grable pose in the mirror, smiling over her shoulder.

Her nails, painted scarlet before her bath, looked shocking against the cups of her bra. She ran her fingers along the lace edge to ensure perfect placement, imagining that they were his possessive fingers, and then smoothed her hands back over the black silk knickers that clung to her round bottom. She continued to think of smooth, fragrant skin as she felt herself grow into her accustomed role and click smoothly into her rightful place and demeanour.

She smiled and applied make-up, the delicate shading and highlighting, relieved that she could put a little more shadow on her eyes now that the dark nights had gathered in. She felt competent while she tipped her head left and right to check her mascara, imagining an evening when she could flirt and laugh and tease. She stood back from her dressing table, her whispering conscience blowing gently at the dusts of powder she left behind, and reached for a simple black dress.

Understated and graceful, it slid over her perfumed body and hid the secretive lace of her underwear beneath flowing lines. Her shoes were satin and slightly too high for her to feel relaxed going down the carpeted stairs so she carried them with her purse when she heard the sound of the door. She slipped them on as she turned the corner to greet the man she adored, the man for whom she had spent hours in preparation.

He smiled when he saw her and breathed her in, resting his lips on her head while she filled the space beneath him. He stroked her shiny long hair and noted the brightest of red nails moments before he kissed her. Then, because she looked so sad when he drew away, he kissed her again.

Finally he straightened his arms to hold her away just far enough that he could have a proper look, and within a heartbeat he saw it. Something was off. He took his time and looked beneath the creams and the shading, past the costume and the charade.

His blue eyes probed, and she kept silent, letting him search, sure that he could not find what was no longer there. She smiled with longing, and when he took her hand and pulled her towards the kitchen chair she licked her bottom lip in anticipation.

Her eyebrows drew in sharply when he pulled her onto his lap. She looked at the floor in silent offering, her knees quivery at the thought of kneeling before him in the way they both enjoyed so much. She frowned in disappointment, and decided that he had broken a man law when he ignored what she was so eager to give.

He looked deeply into her face as if it were a page of fine print, and she wondered what sort of answers he would find there. So she told him the truth – that they had dinner reservations and that she was starving, and then gave him several reasons for their immediate departure, but when she paused to recall the exact nutritional content of her lunch her speech faltered and she fell into the silence that he laid before her like a rug.

He sighed and cleared his throat. 'Are you going to tell me?'

He remained patient while she explained that there was nothing to say, and did he like her nails? And he had no idea how hard it was to get seamed stockings to go straight up the back of a leg. Her delicately constructed façade of gloss and flirtation crumbled, to her great annoyance, and she almost said how mean he was to shatter her good mood. But then she saw such love and consideration in his eyes that she forgot to say anything, and settled into silence once more.

When she started to trace the line of his shirtfront with her finger he knew she was ready to listen.

Her ankles lightly swayed back and forth while he talked, and her teeth gently bit her lower lip. His deep, steady voice stilled her, and despite her fear and shame she felt calm and safe for the first time that day. Truth bobbed up, desperate for air, and her hands reached for it too slowly to hide it from him.

With one finger tracing the buttons on his shirt and her eyes never higher than his collar she told him all of it. It spilt out of her like marbles over the slate kitchen floor, a tale scattered and messy. She looked at the scene in dismay when she finished, certain she had made such a muddle that he would be so flabbergasted he could do nothing except join her in confused silence.

She leaned against his chest, soothed by his hand rubbing small circles on her back, but flicked to alertness when his chest stiffened as though he suddenly realised he had something to do. She recognised his click into activation mode, and thought longingly and hopefully of dinner and restaurants and safe public places.

'Stand up,' he said, so casually she wondered if he might ... but no, he placed a firm hand on her back, and then with just the lightest touch from his other hand he bent her over the table. She gazed at the dark oak, thinking how it was not supposed to be like this.

What happened to the candlelight and witty repartee she counted on and looked forward to all day?

The kitchen was warm and yet when he lifted her dress and laid the dark material gently on her pale back she shivered. The large, bright space, so different from their cosy bedroom, left her open, illuminated, as if she were the one girl in the class who had not done her prep, called out and her shame exposed for all to see. Except there was only him, and that was even worse.

40

His hand rested on her knickers for a moment, causing a flicker of desire within her, a subliminal effect as he seemed to stroke her through the silk. She stayed as still as she could, a show of submission that she wished he saw, her breath stilled in her throat. His practised fingers moved with proficient care as they paused and slowly lowered her knickers, revealing her shaking bottom. Her skin was smooth and fragrant from so much care and he stroked her cheeks gently as he eased the garment down to rest, mingling with the lace at the tops of her stockings.

She hated them resting there. If he removed them completely there would be some sexual element to his actions, a possibility that he might change his mind and make her his own in some carnal manner. This thought kept her head lowered; her desire was shameful and inappropriate. He did not want her that way now. He wanted to spank her like a grown-up little girl, for she was no longer the woman she had tried so hard to be. Her adult attire, her stockings and her silk knickers felt incongruous, a foolish choice for a foolish girl.

Unable to have any impact on any part of herself, she felt small and ashamed. She waited.

Her heels tipped her forward so her bottom pushed high, rudely high. The obscene position brought a blush to her face, and she longed to sit on his lap again, even for a moment. He stepped to her left and she almost

41

reached for him, but her hands refused to move from her mouth, both thumbs tucked between her teeth. She bit hard at the sound of his belt unbuckling.

All she could see was the wood of the table yet she squeezed her eyes shut against the awful noise of whatever he did to prepare the belt to ... do that. The sound was familiar and dreadful, a whisper that made her still throughout.

He explained about her lack of personal organisation that makes life much harder than it needs to be. He explained how he would help her and support her but he could only do so if she told the truth. He explained how lies could never be part of their relationship. All this he said clearly and with metronomic calm so that she would understand and reflect on every word. He was woefully fair.

When asked she replied that she understood, but so softly it was only grace that allowed him to hear her.

The silence in the room broke suddenly despite the solemn preparation. The crack of the belt struck her ears at the same time as the first red pain seared across her cheeks. She breathed in sharply at the shock of it but stayed still as he firmly repeated himself. She could feel the residue of each chastising stroke even as the belt was withdrawn for the next. There was no pause: even between the impacts there was the waiting, a stretching out of fear replaced in an instant with the realisation of pain.

Within moments, her pale cheeks were criss-crossed with angry pink ribbons. She struggled to keep still, pushing the balls of her feet into the slate floor as though they would propel her upwards and away. His stroke was regular, precise, a snap of pain every second as he used a practised eye to measure his efforts. The arms that were strong enough to hold her close and make her feel safe from a scary world were used to good effect as leather, strength and intention merged to make her call out and cry and plead. At first, the sound of the belt on her skin scared her but by the end she could not hear the sound and would not care about it anyway; the simple, pure pain of it was all she knew.

It was some time after she begged him to stop that he stopped.

The moments after were always simple, as there was nothing else to say. He held his arms out and she folded herself into them. They kissed. He held her dress up around her waist, the cool air against her burning bottom. She moved unsteadily from the pain and the shock and from her awkwardness at having her knickers around her thighs, hindering her. She was unaware of how she looked, the hot pink an unplanned addition to her evening's outfit.

So keenly did she hold herself against him that as he sat and pulled her forward over his lap she did not struggle. She clung onto him still, his shirt then his waist and then the legs of his trousers. Her carefully pinned-up hair started to tumble forwards, a blonde message in front of her swollen eyes that more was to come.

It would have been an awkward position had he not held her so tightly. His hard stomach against her side and his firm thighs under her made her feel safe and attached to him. He would not let her fall. He kept her dangling there while her breathing steadied and deepened.

She had submitted long ago and though she did not want any more she accepted it anyway. She trusted him. She was so sore before he started that she cried out at the first blow. He was not gentle, his hand as strong and unremitting as his belt. He covered her with painful prints, each one layered on top of the straight lines his belt had left.

She did not stay still. Her struggle was not lack of submission but rather an automatic reaction to the pain. She had no choice: self-preservation made her buck and kick and cry out as burning pain was added to burning pain.

He was silent as he watched her under his arm and under his hand. He kept up the steady punishment until she started to steady and then slow and finally submit.

This is when he spoke to her.

He talked, punctuating his words with staccato swats of his powerful hand, each one stinging and burning her.

44

He spanked her and talked to her until he could see that she accepted what he said as truth, and then he spanked her until he could feel her give up completely and relax into his love and forgiveness.

Her face was pink when she stood up and her eyeshadow no longer looked sleek. In the bathroom she used cotton wool to take off lines of make-up that had formed rivers down her face. Her hair was simple to fix. Her skin, she noticed as she reapplied lip gloss, looked brighter and clearer than before. Her smile when she left the mirror was shared by her whole face.

Standing before him once again she waited for a kiss and looked at his open hand in confusion. She pouted as she realised what he was asking and took off her panties and handed them to him. She did not pause for breath in her protests as he slipped the flimsy garment into his pocket and held the door open for her to walk through into the crisp autumnal air, the stars bright against the dark blue sky.

At His Bidding
Catherine Paulssen

'Growing up as the youngest of the Ferguson kids meant that whatever you broke was replaced within twenty-four hours. No matter what I trashed – the next day, it had magically returned. Thank you, Daddy!'

Nathan pressed the button and sank back into the pillow. The sound switched off, he continued watching the video of his wife laughing, giggling, looking fondly into the camera as she drank to her father's health on his seventieth birthday.

His spoiled little girl.

His beautiful, beloved, spoiled little girl.

She behaved at their home just as she was used to, growing up as the only daughter of Hollywood's most successful producer, and the youngest sister to four brothers. The house he had bought for them was her realm now, and she was the breezy princess at its centre, expecting things to go her way just as they always had. In a way, he couldn't be mad at her. She simply didn't know better.

A few years ago, in a twist of fate that might have been concocted by her father's scriptwriters, Hollywood's golden princess had fallen for a bright, aspiring law student from Detroit. His hometown wouldn't leave him, no matter how much his circumstances had changed. Never would he forget what it had meant growing up there, in awe of possessing anything worth more than what his father's small salary could buy. Which was pretty much everything.

Growing up like he did meant listening to the cars driving by the bedroom he shared with his brothers and fantasising about owning one of them one day, just one of them. Not the shiny ones, not the big ones. Just any decent American car.

Growing up in Louise's part of the world meant you wrecked a car, one of the shiny cars, the big cars, and had your dad's money buy you a new one.

The other week, she had rushed into the kitchen to have breakfast before going on a shopping spree with her girlfriends. He had been having coffee, engaged in a little chit-chat with Carol, their housekeeper.

'Hey, baby, morning!' Louise pressed a kiss on his cheek.

He clasped his hands around her waist, imbibing her delicious smell. 'Morning, love.'

'Want some cornflakes too?' she asked.

'No, thanks.'

As she turned to kiss him goodbye while putting her bowl of leftover cornflakes down on the kitchen isle, she missed it, and the bowl shattered on the limestone tiles. Without so much as looking at it, she cast a short glance at Carol, who quickly began to clean up the mess.

Louise made to leave without so much as a 'sorry' or a 'thank you'.

'Louise!'

'Huh?' His wife turned around.

'Carol, please give us a minute.'

The housekeeper looked at him with wide eyes. Eventually, she nodded and turned to leave.

'Nathan, I'll be late, so what –' Louise stopped when he grabbed her wrist.

'You're not going until you've cleaned that up.'

'What?'

'I said, you're going to clean that up. You made the mess, you put it away.'

She laughed shortly and gave him a little peck on the cheek. 'I'll see you at dinner.' His hand still held her firmly. 'Let go! You had your fun.'

'I mean it.'

She snorted. 'And I'll be late to meet my friends.'

'Then you better get started,' he gave back calmly.

Something flashed in the glance she threw him. Annoyance? Fascination?

They fought a battle with their eyes for some moments, her catlike emeralds and his glinting dark coals, then Nathan eased his grip on her wrist. A shiver ran through Louise's body. Without saying a word, she got down on her knees and picked up the shattered pieces.

He bent down to fondle the nape of her neck. The little hairs on her skin erected and Louise's body tensed. 'Now you're being a good girl,' he whispered.

She drew in a quivering breath, and got up to throw the fragments into the trash. Avoiding his eyes, she slipped past him out of the room. He heard her grabbing her keys in the entrance hall. Suddenly, her head appeared in the kitchen door. She rushed over to him and kissed him quickly.

'I love you,' she whispered into his ear, and, without looking back once, hurried out of the door.

* * *

Louise's voice drifted to him through the open windows, humming some tune. The slamming of a car door, light footsteps clicking over the cobble stones ... He imagined her small feet in high heels that accentuated the graceful shape of her ankles.

He wanted her. Now.

He was halfway down the grand staircase when Louise entered the entrance hall. She wore a long dress made of pale lavender silk, hugging her curves at all the right places. It was held by buttons above her clavicle and her back. She had combined the designer dress with a cheap, boyish denim jacket that didn't do its exclusivity justice at all.

It was so her.

He cleared his throat. 'I need to talk to you.'

She doffed the jacket and contemplated her husband. For a split second, something in her eyes shimmered. Then she sighed impatiently. 'Fine.'

He waited on the stairs until she was by his side, then followed the waft of the subtle perfume that hit his nostrils as she sashayed past him.

Louise turned one of the bedroom lights on. Goosebumps covered her naked arms, and they weren't induced by the air-conditioning that he always turned up too high. She had seen something in his eyes that intrigued her. Not to mention the unyielding tone of his voice.

'You had another accident with the Cadillac,' Nathan said, leaning on the door frame.

She shrugged. 'Could have happened to anyone.'

His gaze darkened. 'Three times in seven months?'

'You're acting like this because I broke a stupid fence?'

'It's not about the fence. Or the car. You could have hurt someone. You could have hurt yourself.'

'But I didn't.' She stroked his cheek. 'It's just things, Nathan.'

He shook her off. 'You don't get it.'

She rolled her eyes. 'I guess I don't.'

Before she could tell what was coming at her, he had yanked her around and pinned her against the post of their canopy bed. 'In that case ...' He rubbed his hands over her figure, down her hips and up her back. She curled her hands around the wood and held her breath as he undid the button of her left shoulder strap. '... I'll have to teach you.' He kissed her bare shoulder. 'You never got ...' He opened the other strap and the dress's top fell over her chest, exposing her black bra underneath. Nathan traced the shape of her neckline down her shoulder blades. '... a sense of discipline.' He started to open the buttons of her dress behind, gentle, forceful – she couldn't tell.

His breath was hot on her neck, sending tingles all over her body. Nathan traced her hair up to her ears, one hand parting her soft, honey-coloured strands. Very tenderly, he bit her ear's outer shell, then kissed the skin behind it.

She tried to turn, but the grip he had on her made it impossible. Her pulse quickened. The one time he had held her like this had been a few days ago, in the kitchen.

'I ... I don't understand.'

'You will, baby.' He moved to her other ear, kissed it

and blew against the moist spot his mouth had left on her skin. His fingers continued to work on her buttons. 'And Louise?'

'Yes?' It was only a breath.

He leaned forward. 'You'll enjoy the lesson, I promise you that.'

She gnawed at her bottom lip, wondering why his words shot straight to her clit. The last button opened and the silk caressed her skin as it glided down to the ground. She sighed, expecting him to caress her further. Instead, the sateen touch was followed by a forceful stroke of his palm on her bottom. She gasped at the impact. It was barely intercepted by the lace of her panties, but Nathan seemed far from being satisfied. 'Didn't you enjoy that?'

Louise closed her eyes and clenched her fingers tighter around the pole. What had happened right there? And how come it filled her with anticipation instead of anger? And why – why was she that wet already?

Nathan's fingers danced lightly over the panties. They didn't cover her whole butt, and as the pain ebbed away she could feel his finger tracing the tiny curve where her cheeks met the top of her thighs. 'Didn't you, Louise?' he asked again, his voice sharper this time.

She tried to organise the thoughts racing through her head. What did he have in mind? And whatever it was – was she ready for it? What would it do to their relationship? Would it change who they were? Louise braced herself. His voice, albeit stern, was the voice of the man she had fallen in love with and still cherished above all others. The man who knew her better than anybody else. The good sides – and the bad. Maybe it was time to explore a new side of both of them.

'Yes. Yes, Nathan, I did enjoy it.'

His breath caressed her ear and tickled her skin. 'Take off your panties.'

She obeyed and quickly stepped out of the black lace.

Nathan undid her bra and wrapped his arms around her. 'Do you remember our wedding vows?'

A little smile flashed over her face. She let go of the post and turned her naked body towards him. 'I promised to love, to honour and respect you.' She cupped his cheek and let her fingers glide over his skin.

He kissed the palm of her hand. 'And I, to cherish and protect you.'

Their eyes remained locked for a moment, then Nathan took the long pearl necklace she was wearing off her neck and, holding her gaze, bound her wrists with it. 'Hold on to the post.'

Louise swallowed thickly, but did as told.

She waited. His voice finally released her.

'Bend over.'

Of all the commands he had given her in this room – spread your legs for me, rub my dick, rub it harder, say my name – of all the things he had ever asked her to do, this one found her so willing that wanton shame coloured her cheeks light pink. Nathan positioned himself behind her and stroked her bottom.

'You're twenty-eight now,' he stated, and Louise didn't move. 'Twenty-eight years of being spoiled.' He increased the pressure with which he was stroking her cheeks, and all her senses were reduced to the simmering lust that throbbed through her pussy. She got a faint idea of what he was about to do – but he couldn't … he wouldn't … Would he?

He cupped her cheeks in his huge hands. 'You will count. And you will call me sir.' He pressed himself against her and she could feel the bulge in his pants. For a moment, she forgot about what he just ordered her to do, what new world of existing he had instilled in her, but lost herself in fantasising about having his big throbbing cock inside her pussy. His next words brought her back to where he wanted her – under his control, surrendering her whole being to him. 'When you mess up, I will start all over again. Until you have learned the lesson.'

Her body tensed. She was too dizzy, too anxious, too thrilled to reply. Another wave of shame flushed through her body, but there was no denying it: being punished by Nathan for not having been the good girl he expected her to be, the good girl he saw in her – being taught by him how to be that girl – made her body hum with sensations unknown to her until that night.

'Do you understand?'

She nodded. 'Yes.' She cleared her throat. 'Yes, I do.'

Nathan reached around her and covered her breasts with his hands. His fingers stroked her hard nipples. 'You're so beautiful,' he whispered. The loving tone of his voice filled her heart with tenderness for him. So he had heard the very shy shiver of fear in her words. 'Look at you.'

She turned her head and threw a glance at their image in the huge mirror on the other wall. Her sun-kissed skin shimmered underneath his as he stood bent over her, her toned body leaned in a subtle curve against the bedpost. The delicate pearls wrapped around her wrists shone warmly in the dim light. He had given them to her for her last birthday, to complement her beauty – never would she have expected back then that one day he would use them to have her at his mercy.

Her eyes wandered down to that part of her body she knew wouldn't be treated as gently as her nipples, which he rubbed with his thumbs, so lightly it seemed he wanted to tease her all night.

He followed her gaze and flashed his eyes at her. Without saying a word, he brushed a kiss across her flushed cheek and nodded. His hand moved down her back and Louise gritted her teeth.

She had never received so much as a light spank from her parents. Her father had raised his voice at her once, and it was out of worry for her. It was because he cared. She figured that Nathan would spank her for the same reason, that he would punish her because he cared. Because he wanted her to be a better person, a better woman. A better wife.

And a better wife she would be.

Nathan peered at her profile. 'What?'

She looked at him, then lowered her eyes. 'Please spank me.'

His face softened. He lifted her chin with his thumb and kissed her, so tenderly that her tension began to melt away. Still caught in his caress, she didn't even notice the first stroke until it echoed through the silent room and her flesh started to burn.

She clenched her teeth to stop herself uttering the loud groan that built in her throat.

Nathan looked at her expectantly.

'One.' She swallowed. 'Sir.' It sounded strange. And yet, it didn't. Louise couldn't remember, ever in her life, calling someone 'sir'. Yet it felt natural to say it to her husband, her lover, that night.

Her devotion earned her another tender kiss. Nathan took his time with the next slap, but when it came, it was even more exquisite than the first. Louise sucked in the air and couldn't believe the taunt when he didn't pull his hand away but kept it pressed on her maltreated butt, denying it the cool air that would ease its torment.

Numbers three and four left marks of his fingers on her skin, making her all his. She relaxed, despite the anxiety that filled her, anxiety about not knowing if she could take twenty-four more. Anxiety to please him, too. As Nathan continued to slap her, she got used to his force, she learned how to anticipate where she would feel it most, and to savour the moment when the sting vanished to leave her skin all tingly and humming.

Before the next smack landed and the pain bit into her flesh again.

The strokes followed quickly now and, by the time they had reached ten, his rigorous spanking had set her cheeks alight. The pain melted only a moment after his palm hit her flesh, and a sort of satisfying, almost soothing warmth wrapped her burning ass in heated, velveteen pleasure that sent waves of lust through her veins. She knew she was wet as she had never been before.

She spread her legs a little wider, perking up her ass as she did, hoping he would understand the beckoning.

Nathan clasped her waist. She trembled, torn between wanting to be fucked and not wanting him to stop giving her behind the attention she seemed to have been missing all her life, without even knowing it.

'You want me to go harder on you, don't you?' he asked.

She held her breath. His voice had a direct connection

to her clit and, as if on command, more cream wet her pussy at his casually spoken yet incredibly enticing words.

Her nod didn't satisfy him. 'Answer,' he demanded.

A whimper escaped her lips as he fondled her burning cheeks. Could she even fathom what she was wishing for? She closed her eyes. It wasn't hers to decide any more. The irrepressible thrumming of her clit told her what she really needed.

'Please, Nathan ... please ...' Her pleading look met his expectant stare. 'I want to be spanked harder.'

He raised his brows.

'Sir,' she hurried to say. 'Please spank me harder, sir.'

Her trembling lips were sealed with a kiss. 'At your desire,' Nathan murmured as their lips parted. He made a step back, and Louise closed her eyes. The next moment, golden and red sparkles appeared in the darkness. She stumbled, but when the pain blended into tingling pleasure, she let go of her restraints and moaned.

'Eleven, sir,' she groaned. 'Twelve.'

His hands were huge, and they easily spanned her petite bottom. Every forceful stroke sent her against the bedpost, the pearls tingling softly, her flesh groaning. At fifteen, tears stung her eyes, and her hair clung to her shoulders. A little sob interrupted her counting, in spite of herself.

'Shh.' He kissed her dry lips and licked away the little drops of sweat that had formed above her upper lip.

She nodded obediently and clenched her whole body, feeling nothing but her blazing butt, and the incredible wetness between her legs.

'Sixteen, sir.' That one was an almost tender cuff. The next one came all the harder. 'Seventeen.' She enjoyed how he didn't waver, impressed neither by her whimpers nor by the tears running down her face. While she waited for number eighteen to hit her, a naughty voice inside her started to lure. It spoke with the field-tested conviction that she could get everything she wanted from him if she only asked for it the right way. 'That was ... hard.'

'Uh-huh,' he said, his voice level.

She gave him an obedient look from underneath her lashes. 'Maybe ... maybe I could take the rest of my punishment – later? Please?'

Nathan laughed softly. 'That wouldn't be a proper punishment.' His fingers slid from her red hot cheeks between her legs. He found her throbbing clit and circled it lightly. Louise sighed with pleasure. Two fingers, pushed into her pussy, fuelled the desire to be fucked as relentlessly as she had been spanked. It was too tempting to find out how far she could go.

'Please,' she breathed.

'You like it like this,' he commented on her arousal. Her need. 'And, my little princess –' his breath sent shivers along her neck '– you need to learn what it means to be disciplined.'

He quickly withdrew his fingers and smacked her again. 'Eighteen, sir.'

'You will be …'

Another blow hit her. 'Nineteen.' She barely heard her voice any more.

'… rewarded …' He aimed again, then sent her surging against the bed.

'Twenty.'

'… afterwards, if you take your punishment like a good girl.' He slapped her twice.

'Twenty-one. Twenty-two. Sir,' she panted, hoping he would give her a break. And then again, not.

Nathan kissed her neck underneath her ears. 'You know you deserve it.'

'Yes.' She blinked away the fresh tears, but could taste them salty on her lips. 'Yes, sir, I know.'

He wiped her cheek with his thumb. 'I will kiss them away later,' he whispered, his promise as sweet in her ears as the next stroke was painful.

He relentlessly spanked her until they had reached twenty-six. Nathan petted her butt. 'Will you enjoy the last two?'

She nodded, though wincing at the anticipation his words created deep within her. Wincing with thrill and lust that he would increase the severity of his smacks.

'Tell me.'

'I … I will savour them. And I'm hoping – I'm begging you to … to slap me hard, sir.'

'Your wish is my command, my princess.' The tender fondling he treated her ass to while he mumbled those promising words, so deliciously different from the spanking, held her captured. She didn't dare to move.

He didn't disappoint. His next strokes brought her close to fainting with their intensity. She moaned his name, then collapsed, panting, against the bedpost, not before breathlessly uttering the last number – and a devoted 'sir'.

Nathan's arms caught her, and he whispered words of tenderness to her, how proud he was, how brave she had been, how he loved her more than anything else.

She eased her body into his embrace, the showering of his affection soothing her, but in no way appeasing the throbbing between her legs. As he lifted her up to lay her down on the bed, she gave the mattress a doubtful glance. Surely she wouldn't be able to lie or sit anywhere for days without being reminded of the lesson he had given her?

She was right. 'It burns.' She blushed. So did he. Louise loved him for it; that moment, she knew the game they had just discovered had brought them closer. She got up and watched him undress. Piece by piece the body she loved so much was revealed to her, and she couldn't take her eyes off of him. Nathan acknowledged her fixed gaze on his cock with a grin.

'Come here.' He lay down and brushed her waist.

She straddled him. The mere thought of their bodies clashing sent painful stings across her ass. Riding him was not an option. So she shifted nervously until she was sitting over his navel. A drop from the tip of his cock dripped down her butt as his shaft touched her.

Nathan didn't seem to notice, but kept his eyes on her face. 'Higher.' She shuffled up to his chest.

Nathan grabbed her waist tighter, the tips of his fingers almost meeting over her bellybutton. 'Higher, baby.'

'But …'

'Higher.' His eyes flashed encouragingly and she understood. She got on her knees and moved her body until her spread legs were above his face.

'Now that's right,' he said, grinning, and Louise threw her head back with a sigh as his breath hit her swollen clit.

She hissed when his tongue met her flesh. 'Oh baby, please …' She moaned and buried her hands in his curls, doing her best to stay still, to miss none of his sweeps.

For a moment, Nathan withdrew his tongue and ran it over his lips. She was proud to see the appreciation in his eyes. After all, the honey he was tasting was her body's compliment to him. 'Let go.' He kissed her delta. 'I'll manage.'

She looked down at him. 'You're … you're amazing.'

He lapped at her juices and she could see a smile crinkling the corner of his eyes.

'Oh, baby, don't stop. Please don't ...' she murmured, as the heat flaring behind her navel started to spread through her limbs.

He devoured her with every tickle, every kiss, every sucking of his lips. 'I love that,' he murmured, then flicked his tongue over her trembling clit. 'I love you.'

She ran her fingers through her hair and twisted her body. 'And I love you. I love you, Nathan ... oh, baby ... I love you ...' She continued to utter ragged whispers until the tension was released in one loud groan as Nathan made her come.

She flung herself next to him, her limbs still shaken, her legs stiff, her bottom prickling. Fondling his chest, she snuggled her head in the pit of his arm. He turned his head towards her and brushed some sweaty strands out of her face.

Louise beamed at him. Her hand crawled down to his cock, and her petite fingers snaked around it. 'Baby?'

'Mhm.' Nathan bit his bottom lip and moaned softly.

'Tomorrow, I might break one of the vases in the entrance hall ...'

Deportment
Monica Belle

Forty-six Barnstaple Terrace looked much like the houses on either side. The little front garden was immaculate and it seemed to have retained all its original features, but then so had many of the other houses in the road. Certainly there was nothing to hint at its fearsome reputation, and I checked the instructions Miller had given me. My coat covered my clothes, but it was obvious I was trying to conceal something and it was going to be very embarrassing to choose the wrong door. I knew I was stalling too, but I also knew the consequences of being late and quickly started up the path. There was no bell, just a large brass knocker, brightly polished. I knocked, and winced as I saw that my fingers had left marks. Miss Vine was not known for her tolerance, just the opposite.

It seemed to take for ever for the door to open, and when it did I was wishing it hadn't. The woman standing in the doorway could only be Miss Vine herself, nearly six feet tall in her smart old-fashioned heels, straight, slim and elegant, with a double string of pearls setting off a tailored suit in sober grey. Her face was handsome yet stern, her ash-blonde hair twisted up into a tight bun, making it difficult to tell if she was thirty or a well-preserved fifty. In either case she was definitely older than me, but the look in her eyes made me feel as if I were about six and she sixty. I curtsied, as Miller had told me to.

'Good morning, Miss Vine. I think you're expecting me, for ... for my lesson.'

'Come in. So you're Miller's new girl?'

I found myself blushing with sudden pride as I entered a hallway as neat and as old-fashioned as the exterior, and closed the door behind me. Her eyes followed me inside, watching as I took off my coat and hung it on a stand beside several others, including a full-length fur. I now stood revealed in tight red sweater, cream-coloured circle skirt puffed out by petticoats, white socks and ballet slippers. My make-up was correct for the period, the ribbon I'd used to tie off my ponytail the exact shade of my sweater, but her gaze seemed to pick fault after fault, each with an unpleasant consequence. At last she spoke again.

65

'And what is your name?'

'Fudge, Miss Vine.'

'Fudge? I cannot say I entirely approve Miller's habit of giving his girls foolish nicknames, but it does suit you. Yes, soft and sugary, also sloppy, unkempt and several pounds overweight. Can't you even stand up straight?'

I'd thought I was, and immediately tried to adopt the posture Miller had made me practise for so long, even as I struggled to hold back sudden tears, not so much for what she'd said but for the way she'd said it, as if I was barely worthy of her contempt.

'Sorry, Miss Vine.'

'So you shall be, little Fudge, but you will also learn to stand properly, and to walk like a lady, rather than some fat slut trying to attract the attention of a gang of teddy boys, which is the impression you give at present. We had better begin, then. In the study, I think.'

She moved away down the corridor and I followed, now more acutely conscious of my body than of my clothes. I hadn't been sure what to expect, perhaps a dungeon set out with furniture and tools to match her sadistic reputation, perhaps a bedroom with just a couple of implements for my correction, but certainly not the austere yet feminine room I had entered. The walls were panelled in oak to nearly my own height, while the décor was more in keeping with the Victorian age than with the 1950s, let alone modern times. A bookcase occupied much of one wall and a huge shagreen-topped desk another, but the red-and-gold-patterned carpet was entirely clear at the centre, leaving plenty of space. Beside the door was something I'd never seen and hadn't imagined still existed, an umbrella stand apparently made from an elephant's foot. There were no umbrellas in it, but there were canes, dozens of the horrible things, some long, some shorter, some straight, some crook-handled, rattans, malaccas, even a whalebone, but united by showing clear signs of frequent use. I couldn't take my eyes off them, and had begun to shake. Miss Vine's voice was full of quiet amusement as she noticed my interest.

'Yes, Fudge, one or another of those will be applied to your fat little derrière, presently, but there's no need to look quite so frightened. Surely Miller canes you?'

I tried to nod and shake my head at the same time, quite unable to explain how frightened I was of the cane or how Miller used it to keep me on my toes. In the short time we'd been together he'd spanked me more times than I could count, usually just for fun, and used a paddle and a strap in an effort to correct my numerous failings. The cane hung above our bed, ready for use should it be needed, but when the time had come he'd taken me to the point of bending to touch my toes with my bottom exposed, already bare and red from spanking, only to tell me he'd decided to send me to Miss Vine instead.

She seemed mildly amused by my confusion and fear, her lips curved into a faint smile, warm yet cruel at the same time. There was a straight-backed chair behind the desk and she had sat down. A letter lay to one side, on which I could recognise Miller's bold, flowing hand. Curious, I moved a little forward, only to be brought up short by a sharp glance and a sharper word.

'Stop! Stay where you are, Fudge, in the middle of the carpet. Yes, like that. In fact, I think you'd better put your hands on your head, and do try and stand up straight! Goodness gracious, you've barely been trained at all, have you? How long has Miller had you?'

I had adopted the position she'd ordered, making me feel smaller and more ashamed of myself than ever, but I managed an answer.

'Just over three months, Miss Vine.'

She gave a sorrowful shake of her head.

'I suppose it's only to be expected. Miller is a man, after all, and they are simple creatures, with simple tastes. Presumably your so-called training has centred on making yourself available to him for sex? They're like so many satyrs, and he's among the worst.'

Her question didn't need an answer, as my blush gave away the truth of long hours on my knees learning how to use my mouth on his cock and balls, or with my bottom stuck in the air to have my anus stretched, always with the prospect of a spanking if I failed to perform to his expectations. Miss Vine had picked up his letter.

'Indeed, he devotes less space to your appalling posture and general lack of deportment than he does to a certain dirty little habit of yours. I quote: "She can't keep her fingers to herself, always masturbating, even when she's being punished and worse, when she's supposed to be pleasuring me." Really?'

She was looking right at me, with both amusement and disgust, sending the blood to my cheeks, hotter than ever as I stammered out an excuse.

'I ... I can't help it, Miss Vine. I get excited.'

She drew a heavy sigh.

'Yes, he says you are a natural slut, and I can well believe it. Fortunately there is a cure for that sort of behaviour, which can easily be combined with the cure for slouching. Take off your jumper, skirt and petticoats.'

I hastened to obey, scared, but also with a touch of pride as I peeled my jumper off over my head and let my lower garments fall to the ground. If there was one thing she wouldn't be able to criticise it was my underwear: a support girdle, full-cut panties and a cantilever bra, all accurate copies from original designs. Once I'd stepped out of the froth of my petticoats I put my hands back on my head, waiting for a word of approval, or at least acknowledgement. Her face showed only frosty disdain, and when she spoke her voice was sharper than ever.

'Do you know what the word slut means, Fudge?'

'Um … yes, Miss Vine. A slut is an easy girl, a girl who likes sex too much.'

'No, dear. A slut is a dirty, messy girl, a girl with no self-respect. Being promiscuous is only a part of that. You, Fudge, are a slut. Now fold your clothes!'

I jumped back at the sound of her voice, but tried to obey as quickly as I could, only to catch my toe in my petticoats. For one awful moment I was hopping on one foot, desperately trying to keep my balance, before I went down, landing on my knees with my bottom in the air before managing to scramble up once more. Miss Vine had put one hand over her eyes in a gesture of despair, adding to the heat of my blushes as I sorted myself out. Only when I was back in the middle of the carpet with my hands on my head did she speak again.

'I can see I have my work cut out here. Right, put your hands down, folded in your lap.'

She'd got up as she spoke, to walk briskly to the cane stand. My stomach went tight as she began to search among them, and tighter still as she selected the whale-bone, which looked to be the most vicious of them all. I wanted to speak, to tell her I'd never been caned before, to beg her not to beat me too hard, to offer any lesbian delight she cared to name if only she'd let me off. But

Miller had told me the consequences of disobedience or of making a fuss, and I stayed silent.

Miss Vine had gone to the bookcase, where she selected a thick leather-bound tome. I thought she was going to read from it, no doubt some moral passage to stress my faults, and was surprised when she placed it on top of my head. My body stiffened by instinct and I managed to balance the book, earning my first words of praise.

'Good girl. Evidently you are not completely useless. Now, shall we see if you can keep it there while you receive your chastisement?'

'Yes, Miss Vine.'

She'd come behind me and I desperately wanted to see what she was up to, but knew the book would fall off if I turned my head. That was sure to make my punishment worse still, not that I had any idea what I was going to get, or if I could take the pain of the hideous strip of polished whalebone at all. My only comfort was my choice of panties, which encased the cheeks of my bottom with a double layer of heavy cotton to protect my skin. Then she took hold of the waistband and inverted them around my thighs.

'I don't suppose a girl like you understands the shame of being made to go bare bottom, but I am sure you will appreciate how much more it will hurt.'

'Yes, Miss Vine.'

A single hard tug and my panties were pulled down

to my knees, where they stayed, a tangle of white cotton to make my exposure more blatant still. She was wrong about my not understanding the shame of my exposure, for my blush was growing deeper and hotter in the knowledge that my bare bottom and the triangle of fur covering my sex were on show to her, but I didn't dare voice my feelings.

The cane touched my bottom and I winced. I felt the book start to slide, made a grab for it and pushed it back onto the top of my head just in time. Miss Vine ignored the incident and tapped the cane across my cheeks again. This time I managed to keep the book on my head, and I told myself I'd stay perfectly still as the cane lifted from my flesh. A sob of fear escaped my lips and I was fighting back my need to speak as she appeared right at the edge of my vision, but I held back until the cane hit.

I heard the whistle and the book was already falling from my head before the thin whalebone rod smacked into my flesh, to set me screaming and totally out of control for an instant before I was jumping up and down on my toes and clutching at my bottom, as I babbled out a mixture of curses and apologies that ended in a single, plaintive sob. Miss Vine drew a heavy sigh.

'I guessed as much. You're a clown, Fudge. What are you?'

'I'm sorry, Miss, but that hurt so much!'

'What are you?'

'A clown, Miss Vine. I'm sorry.'

'Yes, a stupid, clumsy, fat-bottomed clown. Now pick the book up.'

* * *

I stood rigidly to attention, my hands by my sides, my back straight, the hateful book poised on top of my head, nude, sweaty and dishevelled. My bottom and thighs were criss-crossed with welts, some new, some from the week before, some from my first visit. Every single cut had made me drop the book every time, for the simple reason that the pain of a cane stroke made my muscles jerk by instinct.

Miss Vine hadn't given up, but she had slowly lost her poise. She now stood by me, in a skirt of light pale-yellow wool, but with her jacket off. The top three buttons of her blouse were undone, showing off a surprisingly generous slice of cleavage, while her sleeves were rolled up to her elbows. Her fine blonde hair was still in a bun, but less tight than before, with wisps escaping around her neck and temples. She seemed younger than I'd thought, while her expression seemed less stern than frustrated, even nervous, as was her voice.

'For goodness' sake, Fudge, do try! It's really not that difficult!'

'Sorry, Miss Vine.'

She blew out her breath and glanced at the handsome clock on the mantelpiece, then shook her head as she addressed me once more.

'Hold still. Here it comes.'

The cane whistled down and cracked across my cheeks one more time. My muscles jerked and the book fell off, to land on the floor with a thump. It was beginning to get a bit ragged at the edges, and the spine showed some damage, although far less than my poor bottom. I had learnt a lot during my three visits to her, including how to bring another woman to orgasm with my tongue, but most of the time had been spent trying to balance the book on my head while I was caned. My repeated failures had amused her at first, then made her annoyed, but now she seemed close to panic, which I didn't understand at all.

'Put it back on your head, you stupid girl! Oh, God.'

She glanced at the clock again, just as the bell went. I reached for my clothes, neatly folded on a chair to one side, but Miss Vine brought me up short.

'Do you really think that it matters if you're in the nude? It's Miller.'

'It is?'

She ignored me as she made a few hasty adjustments to her own clothing and hurried to the door, leaving me wondering what was going on. Miller always took full advantage of the state I was in when I got home from my sessions with Miss Vine, but he hadn't said anything about joining us. It was him, though, his deep, confident voice unmistakable as he greeted Miss Vine, calling her Emily and kissing her before coming into the study. By then I was back in the middle of the carpet with the book once more balanced on my head, determined to show I was a good girl in front of my Lord and Master. That didn't mean I was going to be able to keep the book on my head, though, and I wondered if I'd shortly be getting a naked spanking in front of Miss Vine, or perhaps be made to suck his cock while she watched. I stayed stock still as they entered the room, but managed to speak.

'Good morning, Master.'

He stepped close, to walk around my naked body, admiring the welts that decorated my bottom and both sides of my thighs before he spoke.

'Good morning, Fudge. I see Emily has been hard at work, but has she succeeded, that is the question? I'll grant that you're better at keeping your fingers off your sticky little cunt while you suck me, but what about the book?'

Miss Vine had stayed by the door rather than going to her desk and seemed more nervous than ever as she answered him.

'She can do it, but she's already had twelve cuts today, so perhaps next week?'

It was an open lie, as I'd only had seven and the book had fallen off every time, and there was no doubting the note of panic in her voice. Miller reached out to stroke the flesh of my bottom before he replied.

'No, we should stick to our agreement, don't you think? Which cane have you been using? Something thin, to judge by the welts. Your whalebone?'

Miss Vine had put it back in the stand when she left the room, but Miller retrieved it and inspected the long, wicked length of polished bone as he threw her a questioning glance. She gave a single, very nervous nod.

'Yes, I judged it most effective.'

'Oh, undoubtedly. Now then, let's see how you've done. Shall we say, best of three?'

Miss Vine didn't answer, but, to my astonishment, as she stood back against the door she was struggling not to pout. Miller didn't seem to notice but gave the whalebone an experimental swish through the air, then stepped behind me to tap the evil thing across my cheeks as he spoke.

'Right, Fudge, you're to do your best, just as Emily has taught you.'

He brought up the cane and held it high for a long moment before whipping it down across my bottom. I yelped and jerked, as always, completely unable to control my instinctive reactions. The book fell off. As I bent to pick it up I saw that Miss Vine had closed her eyes, and that her hands had started to shake. Miller spoke quietly.

'One down. And again …'

I'd already put the book back in position and he didn't wait, but whipped the cane smartly down across my bottom with the same inevitable result. As the book hit the floor Miss Vine let out a weak sob, and when Miller spoke again his voice was tinged with amusement.

'Oh, dear. That's not good at all, is it, Emily? Never mind, I'll give you one last chance. Do try and stay still, Fudge.'

'Yes, Master.'

I did my best, but I knew it was hopeless even before I'd got the book properly balanced once more. When the cane bit into my cheeks my muscles jerked and the book fell off, as always. I had managed to stifle my scream, though, and kept my hands off my bottom, but I knew it wasn't enough and quickly hung my head in anticipation of further punishment. Miller gave a low chuckle and shook his head before speaking again.

'Hopeless, really quite hopeless.'

I thought he was talking to me but Miss Vine responded, her tone almost pleading.

'It's not my fault! She's … she's the one who's hopeless! I've never known such a clumsy girl, and she can't handle pain at all.'

He reached out to stroke my hair as he replied.

'I know, that's why I love her, because even a playful little spanking makes her wriggle about like a piglet with mustard up its arse. Nevertheless, Emily, a deal's a deal. I trust you'll keep your word, just as I would have done had you succeeded.'

Miss Vine lifted her chin, but there was a quaver in her voice.

'Of course. Fudge, you may leave the room.'

Miller shook a finger.

'Uh, uh, Fudge stays. This will be an important part of her training.'

I'd been about to leave the room, and hesitated, but Miss Vine had hung her head as if in defeat, and when Miller snapped his fingers and pointed to the chair in which I'd piled my clothes I went to sit down, gingerly lowering my aching bottom on to the soft cotton of my panties. Miss Vine stepped to the centre of the carpet, where I'd stood so often, and as she picked the book up I finally realised what was going to happen. My mouth fell open in astonishment as she placed the book on her head, her face frozen save for a tell-tale flicker at one corner of her mouth, her body perfectly straight and perfectly still, even as Miller began to adjust her clothing, and to talk to me.

'You see, Fudge, girls like Emily love to be in control and they love to inflict pain, especially on other girls, but I've yet to meet one who doesn't have a deep, secret desire to have her own little bottom warmed just the way she likes to warm others. Isn't that true, Emily, my sweet?'

Miss Vine didn't respond, remaining in statue-like immobility even as he tucked her skirt into its own waistband. Her slip followed, her panties were pulled down and her trim little bottom was bare to the room, to Miller, to myself and to the cane. He carried on, still addressing me.

'It is true, take my word for it. Perhaps, just possibly, there are some women who genuinely never fantasise about having a man take them to task with a good spanking, or perhaps a nice dirty blowjob, but Emily here is not among their number. Oh, no, she accepted my little bet, three hundred pounds against having to prove she can do what she's been trying to train you for, and she lost.'

As he finished he brought the cane around in a long, swift arc, whistling through the air to crack down across Miss Vine's naked bottom with every bit as much force as she'd ever used on me. I saw it hit, saw her flesh quiver and watched the cane lifted to leave a thin white line that rapidly turned to a set of scarlet tramlines just like those decorating my own bottom. Yet she never so much as flinched, only a brief flicker of her eyes betraying her pain and the awful shame I knew she'd be suffering from what she'd said to me so often. I was briefly seized with pity at the thought, then with an emotion quite new to me, a cruel, vengeful delight that seemed to go straight to my sex.

Miller grinned as if reading my mind, then gave her another stroke. Again, only a brief closing of her eyes gave away her inner feeling, but I had no such reserve. My mouth was still wide, my eyes too, while my nipples had begun to pop out. With the third stroke I was fighting the urge to slip a hand between my legs, despite all the effort Miss Vine had put into making me control my nasty little habit. Still the book remained balanced on her head, and after four, and five, by which time I'd given in to my rising arousal. Miller saw, and laughed.

'You don't need to do that, Fudge.'

I made a face and pulled my hand away from between my thighs just as he gave her the sixth stroke, harder than ever. Finally her reserve began to crack, her knees buckling slightly, but she kept her upper body rigid and the book stayed on her head as Miller went on.

'You don't need to do that, Fudge, because ...'

He brought the cane down again, not on her bottom but across the back of her thighs and even harder than before. She screamed, jerked, and the book fell to the floor with a final dull thump, to leave her sobbing and gasping as she fell to her knees, her hands reaching back to clutch at her smarting cheeks. Miller gave a contented sigh, then turned to me once more.

'Because, Fudge, darling, Emily is going to do it for you, aren't you?'

There was a harsh edge to his final words, but it didn't

seem necessary. Miss Vine had already begun to crawl towards me on her hands and knees, her well-whipped bottom lifted for Miller's inspection as he pulled down his fly to release his cock, her cunt ready behind as she buried her face between my legs.

Compensation
Rachel Randall

'You'll have to do better than that.'

Dana slaps her hand down, open-palmed, to make her point. And it's because she's leaning forward – stretched across sacrosanct, employee-only air space – that she catches his reaction.

His pupils spread. His breath hitches. His lips part, but he doesn't offer another meaningless apology. He doesn't say anything at all.

Her irritation, which has been climbing steadily during the hours of her delayed flight, pauses its ascent. Intrigued, she curls her fingers against the counter, pressing hard until their tips pale from the pressure. She sees him notice the fine lines of her scars, badges of two decades spent in kitchens, before he ducks his head away from her stare. When he clears his throat, it's a flustered sound – the first time since she reached the front of this line that she's managed to shake anything genuine out of him.

She smiles at him; it's been hours since she last used those muscles. 'This is the third time in a month your airline has –' she pauses deliberately, pushing, pushing the moment until he looks up at her again '– fucked me.'

He colours. Heat spreads blotchy across his face, turning him from a generically handsome young man into someone of greater interest.

It's been a trying day. A delayed-now-cancelled flight. She's been passed from counter to counter. They help without helping, she thinks. Experts in customer service cockblock. It's not something she puts up with in her restaurant, and it's infuriating to deal with it here.

'I'm sorry,' he says. His voice trembles, just slightly, and he darts his gaze down to where her hands are still resting across that invisible boundary, infringing on his space.

Something rings true about the words this time. He's sincere beyond the corporate script. They're in the middle of a bustling airport, but there's no mistaking how he's just laid himself bare. She slides her hands across the counter, scratching her fingernails along where his shirt cuffs have drawn back above his wrists. In her wake, dark hairs rise rigid across his exposed skin.

He leans closer on a held breath, leaving no question

in his mind. He's up for it. Which is why she tells him, instead of wasting time asking, 'I'm owed compensation.'

There's a mother with two children nearby. They're not close enough to hear, but they're still making him edgy. Not an exhibitionist, she thinks, but without disappointment. There are plenty of other possibilities.

'The airline –'

'From you. You're going to make this better for me. Tonight.'

He nods vigorously, his expression almost painfully vulnerable. She can see how eager he is to be of use to her after all, how pleased he is to be noticed, and, underneath it all, how greedy he is.

Tasty, she thinks, hungry herself, and that's why hours later, she sits at the bar in the best of the airport hotels, nursing her drink and a full-body arousal.

When he finally slides onto the stool beside hers, she makes him wait five minutes before she acknowledges him. She's trying his patience in the same way his employer has tried hers; she's testing to see how much he likes the steely disapproval in her voice.

'I expected you earlier,' she tells him.

His voice is hoarse. 'I'm sorry.'

'You say that so often. But are you ready to show me how sorry you are?'

'Can I ... I want to buy you a drink.'

Up close and personal, she can see that he's very pretty, even in the airline uniform she's spent the better part of the day hating on sight. He must be a good ten years younger than her. And willing.

'So buy me a drink,' she replies, and at his grin she wonders how far down the scale of positive reinforcement she'll have to slide before that happy expression goes blank with lust. She tests him, pitching her tone fiercer than before. 'Convince me to stay.'

They wait in loaded silence until the bartender passes her a new beer, cold vapour still rising from the mouth of the bottle. She sucks its grooved rim and enjoys the way her young man shifts on his stool, deliberately bunching the fabric of his uniform trousers. She can't see anything, but she can imagine.

'So ... you're travelling on business?'

Small talk. Bless him. 'I own a restaurant. I have investors, suppliers. And you're wasting my time again.' She sets the drink down. 'Compensation,' she says, drawing out the syllables. 'Can you deliver?'

'Ask me for anything.' His accent is smudging as he gets more excited, the regulation English turning more regional.

She wets her lips. 'I want a room upgrade at this hotel.'

'Already done. Your luggage has been moved already.'

He's smug now on top of that excitement. Riding a wave of self-satisfaction because he's anticipated what she'd ask for.

'Presumptuous,' she notes, 'but well done. How many favours do you owe the concierge?'

He can't meet her stare.

'Good boy.' A glance downward shows that not even the fabric of his trousers can hide a very promising bulk. 'An upgrade to business class on my flight tomorrow, and access to the Club Lounge on my next trip.'

'Yes ... all right.'

'What, will you sneak into the database now that you're off duty?'

'We all do it.'

'Naughty.' She studies his hands. Long fingers, clenched around his pint glass. How will he try to touch her? 'One more thing – a very, very good bottle of champagne in that room you've booked for us.'

The promise of 'us' doesn't appear to register as quickly as the proposed expense. 'Penance should hurt a little,' she chides him at his wince. 'I'd hate for you to go home feeling guilty about how you treated me today. Go on, ask your concierge friend.'

He bites his lip but nods.

Dana decides she likes his special blend of swagger and submission very much. She supposes that he's done this before, with other women, maybe even a few men as well. She likes the thought of it, that beneath the façade of professional courtesy and blushing kink is this obediently slutty side of him.

Taking her time with the rest of her drink, letting things simmer, she watches him speak with the concierge out in the lobby. She wonders whether there's a going rate for such negotiations, and if she's coming out on the expensive side.

The marble of the expansive, expensive lobby is so glossy she can see her face in it. As she crosses to him, he watches avidly and his intensity puts a spring into her tired step. The marble clatters underneath her low heels; it's an authoritative noise that follows them as he breaks away to join her. He's brandishing a shiny gold keycard, heading for the bank of elevators, but she plucks it from his fingers as she strides on past to the stairs.

She doesn't look behind her to make sure he's following – he will be. And sure enough, his footsteps are even thuds while she takes the steps two at a time.

He calls out her new room number but says nothing else until they reach the door. Then he offers, 'My name's –'

'Hush,' she chides him, spidering her fingers up his cheap tie to the knot, then letting them slide down again and away. His name badge reads Denton and it's part of the fun that she won't ask what he goes by in his off-hours. 'I'm much more interested in what else you plan to do for me.'

The low buzz of the keycard activating the lock nearly covers his soft sigh, but not quite. She feels the stretch of her mouth curving with delight. Lights flicker on when she jams the keycard into the slot on the wall. This trophy room is much bigger than the original she's abandoned – the bed alone is twice the size.

She takes it all in while he carefully shuts the door behind them. 'Kiss me,' she orders. She knows she has to strike hard and fast before uncertainty gets the best of him.

She lets him brush their lips together, just a tingling touch, but when he tries to deepen it she pushes heavily at his shoulder. Not back, not away, but down.

'I meant,' she says, impatient at the need to clarify, 'kiss me, on your knees.'

He sinks to the carpet. She kicks off her heels, bringing him into alignment with his goal. The obstacle of her skirt is one that he conquers by pressing his mouth to where her pussy throbs beneath the fabric. It's a simple solution, more elegant than fumbling at her thighs, but nowhere near as satisfying.

'Make me naked,' she commands. They're moving fast, but she's confident he'll handle it.

He swallows, blinking at her with dark, lust-blown eyes. His hands are clumsy but he manages to improvise by pulling her skirt up around her hips. Her knickers are soft, lacy cotton, and he scowls at them in concentration before thumbing thoughtfully along the inner elastic.

She jerks her chin, granting permission, but he doesn't

immediately move his hands from where he's splayed them on her thighs. If this were her kitchen, she'd rap his knuckles with a spoon if he hesitated like this over a pan. Here, she has to content herself with tangling her fingers into the curly hair of her novice and yanking.

He mouths her again, this time with just the one layer between his open lips and her skin. Her clit starts to stiffen under the damp heat of his breath.

'Naked, I said.' She shoves her knickers down and off; her knuckles brush the pout of his lips. 'Good customer service means never having to ask for something twice.'

'I'm sorry.'

The best part is, he feels sorry. His breath comes hotter, faster, now he's just a whisper from pressing his mouth to her bare skin. Her skirt bunches awkwardly, blocking her view. She thinks about pushing him away so she can shimmy it off, but he takes his first, tentative lick of her and the thought shivers into nothing.

With other lovers, she's taken the time to teach them what she likes, to find out how that mixes with their preferred play. With Denton, she feels selfish, and her solipsism is such that she doesn't wish him to know her body's secrets. He's promised her compensation, after all. It's his debt to repay, not hers; her satisfaction tonight should be duty free.

So she enjoys his best efforts, guiding with broad directives instead of a detailed recipe. She feels herself grow wet, wetter, under his lapping tongue. His kneeling posture is awkward – he's too tall to be folded comfortably at her feet – and she gives him only brief chances to haul in breath. He doesn't seem to mind.

'You tart,' she murmurs, rubbing her palm against his scalp. He whimpers against her pussy and the vibrations incite her to rub again, wanting more.

Now he's found a rhythm, a stuttering thrust of his tongue into her slick folds, that's enough to make her lose her edge. She shoves her pelvis against his mouth as the first real zing of orgasmic intent makes her clit go rigid. He sucks it into his mouth, moaning a little around her. He's much better at this than she expected; it makes this entire awful day worthwhile. The noises he's making alone …

'Get on the bed,' she orders. 'Shoes and jacket off, leave the rest.'

Denton obeys with an eagerness that makes her smirk. As she stalks towards him, shedding the last of her clothing, she notices her arousal glossing his chin. There's a spot of her cream at the corner of his mouth, and it's a sweet garnish to the way he's watching her curves.

The champagne is already set out on the table by the window. Dana ignores the flutes in favour of the bottle itself. She strips off the foil with expert ease, and enjoys the way he monitors her hands' movements along the bottle's long neck. The pop of the cork doesn't so much break the tension as build it.

She goes to the bed and kneels easily, with one foot on the floor taking her weight. The champagne swings from her hand as she studies him. She says, 'Unbutton your shirt,' and he does. His chest is smooth and lightly muscled. Pale in a way that screams, 'Mark me.'

She says, 'Give me your tie,' and he does. He tries to prolong the contact of her fingers, but she sways the icy bottle dangerously close, and he pulls away quickly before the cold glass makes contact.

She says, 'Show me your cock,' and he flushes, all that pale skin of his chest mottling with humiliation-excitement-arousal. 'Slowly,' she orders. Then he does: a release of the top button, an inching down of his zip. He's wearing boxer briefs, distended by his erection, and it's more than enough of him to whet her appetite.

The zipper creeps down, down, and she judges her moment carefully, commanding him to stop just before the teeth crest the curve of him. His hips jerk, his cock seeking friction and finding only restrictive pressure. The zip creaks in protest, but holds.

Now she crawls to loom above him, just to let him think she might kiss him. She tilts the bottle instead. Champagne fizzes, slicking his throat and bubbling into the notch of his collarbone. His nipples peak in reaction, and he flinches underneath her bracing hand on his sticky chest. She sets the bottle on the bedside table, scenting the sharp sweetness of the alcohol mingling with his musk and wanting a taste of both.

She runs her forefinger through the splashes of champagne, slicking up the pad before popping it in her mouth to suck. It's an *amuse bouche* that makes them both groan. Dana wonders if it's the decadent visuals, the pornographic scenario, or the dominant clamp of her calves around his hips that's doing for him. All three are working very well for her.

His eyelids droop to half-closed and his mouth falls open. When she guides his hands above the pillows he keeps them there without fuss, flexing only as she winds his tie in a loose knot around them.

She surveys her handiwork. 'I'm going to touch myself now,' she tells him. 'And you won't move your hands from where I've put them. You'll wait for me, like your airline made me wait.'

He whines.

She smiles down at him. 'I'll let you come – when I'm ready.' Sitting back on her haunches, she revels in the restless shake of his legs underneath her body. Then she slides her hand between her legs.

He strains against her. His necktie binds his hands, but it would take no effort at all to shrug it off. He's held in place by the force of his want alone. He can get up and leave, if he doesn't like this game. He so clearly doesn't want to leave.

Dana's fingers rub through the folds of her pussy, putting on a show that he gives fierce attention. Watching him, she wonders how he first discovered his kinks, and what he likes best about picking up women like her. She's reminded of a well-worn thought – how do airport employees feel about being left behind while everyone else leaves? For a moment she's tempted to ask, then it strikes her that tonight is her answer. He finds his adventures closer to home.

She palms her sex, giving herself a bit of pressure because he's not the only one enjoying himself. And if her fingers slip inside, neither of them is going to protest …

'Are you comfortable?' she purrs. 'I'm very comfortable.'

His hips buck and in reply she slides her fingers so they rub across her rough inner wall. With her free hand, she dabs champagne off his chest then circles her clit in quick little motions. She can feel how plump it is. Her clit liked his tongue and this luxurious teasing is fattening it further. She looks down at the thick cock straining against his trousers and presses harder into her pussy.

She imagines how he must feel right in this moment. Made to wait, growing harder. Longing to touch her skin. Desperate to fuck. They'll fit together so well when he sinks deep …

'Condoms?' she asks.

His hips jolt again, and his zip threatens to pop. 'My jacket.'

Humming, she moves off him and reaches down to pick it up off the floor. The second she's gone, she hears the loud shift of his movements against the mattress. She spins around to find his trousers wriggled down past his hips. The blue cotton of his briefs skims his swollen penis like a second skin, showcasing a sleek wet spot.

Her breath catches. At his disobedience, of course.

Dana leans across him, letting her breasts sway near to his face as she unwraps his hands and tosses his tie away. His fingers twitch towards her until he manages to get himself under control. She arches an eyebrow in acknowledgement.

'That's right. No touching.' She leans further – very close – and lets her nipple graze his collarbone. Goosebumps ripple across his skin. She touches her tongue to his throat and tastes champagne overlaying the salt of his skin.

She straightens, taking her time. 'Naked. Now.'

He's learned since earlier; he doesn't wait to be asked twice. And perhaps he's naïve enough to imagine that she'll give his poor behaviour a pass.

With him bare, all she can focus on is his cock, rising rigid from wiry curls. He has a good curve and the head is heavy and flushed dark. Her mouth waters as a thin line of pre-come seeps from the slit. Yes, she wants him very badly, but not so much as he needs correction.

'On your knees.'

He immediately turns over. His cock bobs, drawing her eyes away from the lean line of his back. The textures of vertebrae and muscle tempt her to lick, but instead she pours champagne onto the palm of her hand and takes hold of his ball sac. She rolls his testicles, considering, then tugs a little until his breath releases in an explosive gasp.

He cries out when she lets go.

'You're disappointed?' she chides. 'Think of me. That's twice you've disappointed me.'

The hotel is five-star, new since they redid the airport. Its many amenities are listed in a gilt-edged black book by the bedside, one that's just thick enough to feel heavy when she weighs it in her hand. If she were without entertainment she would have spent a good half-hour insulting the room service offerings before heading down to the restaurants to sample their best. But tonight she has a better use for the menu in mind.

Her first whack catches him unaware. His body clenches up, his breath choking out of him. The cheeks of his buttocks tense.

'Wha–?'

She slaps him again, a backhand with the book, and he yelps but doesn't ask any more questions.

'Tell me if you want me to stop.'

His breathing is harsh between them, but not laboured. Not yet.

'More,' he groans. 'I ... deserve it.'

She exhales on a wave of pure lust, then steadies herself. 'This is for asking me how you could help when you knew full well you couldn't do a bloody thing.'

She whacks him, the sound ringing through the room. Broken capillaries mark her place. He squirms lower onto his elbows, thrusting his ass up into the air.

'And this is for touching yourself when I explicitly told you not to.'

The sensation of contact judders perfectly through her arm, making her gasp as he shouts, 'Yes!'

She plants a kiss in the centre of Denton's shoulder blades. His ass is reddened, with little scratches from the stiff leather edges of the book. It's immensely satisfying to look at, even better to touch. She brushes gentle fingertips over the blazing hot skin.

'There,' she murmurs. 'I think that should satisfy European Union airline regulations, don't you? Or shall we write to Brussels and recommend a few additions to the passengers' bill of rights?'

She's aching between her legs now – no longer an itch of anticipation or the slow heat of making him wait, but real need. Hot and dirty.

'Turn over.'

His condom is ribbed, and slick with its own lube, not that she needs it. She's so wet that she can feel her thighs gliding together before she spreads them. Straddling him, Dana eases down, letting her bottom brush over his groin until he's arching up and grabbing at her hips to hold her in place. She swats his hands away then grabs him by the wrists and pulls his arms back up above his head. His fingers hook obediently into the fabric of the pillowcase.

'Stay, this time,' she orders him, breathless.

It's a test for him when she rolls the condom down. She takes her time about it so she can savour the shape and feel of him. He quivers beneath her, and her thighs strain with the effort of holding herself still above him.

The heat between their bodies is acting as a magnet, pulling at her, encouraging her to lower herself and grind against that glorious cock. He's warmed up now, nicely spanked and punished. No reason not to –

She's done with waiting. Just fists him into place and rubs his glans against her swollen pussy, watching him all the while. Reddened face, eyes screwed shut. Mouth moving soundlessly and knuckles white against expensive sheets.

'Yeah, like that,' she murmurs, and sinks.

There's blunt pressure then the glide of his thick shaft into her body. He goes deep, right away, and she rises up quickly so she can revel in the drag of him against her clutching walls. She does it again and again, sinking and rising, denying him the satisfaction of directing his own strokes.

Using him as her sex toy.

He's incoherent beneath her, shifting and rolling his hips. His cock rubs in a new way, making sparks dance across her vision. More of that, she decides, and uses her hands to urge him on. She rubs one palm along his chest, enjoying the stiffness of his nipples, and uses the other to hook him up to her for a kiss.

Her tongue slicks up the seam of his lips. His mouth against hers is lush and exciting. He's pliant underneath her now, following her lead. The faint stubble of a long day scratches at her cheek with enough bite to make things spicy. His bottom lip feels good against her teeth as she lets herself fall into him.

They both grunt as her weight rides him deeper into her. Now she's lying across him, her hair sticking to his chest. At this angle she can squirm back onto his cock as she likes. His hairy thighs scratch against her skin, and at his groin there's fantastic friction for her clit. It's … not going to take long.

And it doesn't. Her orgasm begins as a slow burn – the pressure of him on exactly the right spot inside her, their grinding, the taste of his nipples underneath her panting mouth. Then it speeds up, fasterfaster, until she's slamming back onto him, harder and harder, so she can get off exactly how she wants.

'Take it. Yes. Yes – Fuck.'

She convulses around him as her tension releases.

As soon as her orgasm squeezes her control away, his hands rush down from above their bodies to knead her ass. He spins them over and his hips slam against hers in urgent thrusts that send her spiralling again. Then he freezes, taut, and shudders against her, coming helplessly into her.

Everything is warm and wet between them. The very last remnants of an unpleasant day have been utterly banished. When she's got her breath back, she'll decide whether or not to admit that to him.

Denton reaches between them and gets rid of the condom with unsteady fingers. He looks so sweet in the moment that she rises up on her elbows and draws him back to her. Their kiss is slow and delicious, and reminds her that she still hasn't properly tasted his cock.

'I've got an early flight,' she says, a warning to herself as she can't help but dig her nails into his hip.

'And I've got friends who can fast-track you through security,' he points out. His voice is scratchy from moaning, and she can see her teethmarks on his reddened lip.

Dana's never been one to say no to dessert. She reaches for the champagne. 'In that case,' she says, 'let's explore how many other ways you can say you're sorry.'

April Is So Annoying!
Giselle Renarde

'Hey, boss.' April smacked Rick on the ass and laughed raucously at his stunned expression. 'Look at that grin! You got laid last night, didn't you?'

When Rick just stared at her, dumbfounded, Heather stepped in, scolding. 'April, mind your manners!'

Heather glared at the little bitch Rick had inexplicably hired without consulting her. What the hell was he thinking? This chick was nuts.

Rick finally spoke up to say, 'April, you need to be more professional if you want to work here.'

'So I guess that's a no, eh?' April snickered, and already Heather'd had too much of that annoying laugh, like a cross between a high-pitched donkey's bray and a snoring anteater. They couldn't possibly keep her on staff. Heather had never taken such an immediate and all-encompassing dislike to anyone. Ever.

Thankfully, April sauntered off to restock the buffet without another word, waggling her hips like a waitress in a 50s diner. Could she not see how much effort Heather had expended to infuse a little class into this brunch restaurant? How obtuse could a person be?

Heather turned to Rick and growled. 'That girl's out of control. Already, she's said to an elderly couple that we should combine the words "brunch" and "restaurant" to call the place a "breastaurant". Thank God they laughed. Then she told an overweight lady to go easy on the bacon! That didn't go over so well.'

'I'm sorry. I didn't know she'd be like this.' Rick watched April dump the half-full tray of hash browns in with the scrambled eggs. 'Christ, she can't do anything right, can she?'

'Not that I've seen.' Heather prided herself on her calm nature and pleasant demeanour, but with April around she just couldn't contain her agitation. 'I can't wait tables when I'm putting out fire after fire with the customers, Rick. Your restaurant, your hire, your problem.'

'I'm sorry,' he repeated, but she'd forgiven him already. She never could stay mad at Rick – especially not when he raised an eyebrow and said, 'Hey, do you think I should have told April the truth about this weekend?'

Rick's grin, though somewhat churlish, was so irresistible Heather wanted to kiss him there and then. But she wouldn't let herself do it, not at work. They never let on around the restaurant that they were knocking boots after hours – lead server and owner was just too obvious a pairing.

'Why on earth did you hire her?' Heather had to ask. 'She's not even pretty. I can't spot one redeeming quality in that train-wreck.'

Rick shrugged. 'She was a little weird in the interview, but her references were top-notch.'

'All wanting to see the back of her, I imagine.' Heather rolled her eyes as April tried to balance a fruit platter on her head and hula dance for a Polynesian family. 'Put that down this second!' Heather felt like a kindergarten teacher, and she looked to Rick for help. When he just laughed, she stormed over to set April straight.

The day went downhill from there. Just when Heather figured things couldn't get any worse, April started asking patrons, 'Are you a top or a bottom?' and, for those who didn't understand the question, she provided an in-depth explanation.

Heather was so busy running around the place like a chicken with its head cut off, apologising and offering free coffee, free pancakes, free anything, she didn't even notice when poor Mr Patel came in. He and his wife had been regulars for as long as she could remember. Even close to the end, when the chemo had taken his wife's hair and everything tasted like cardboard, they'd still come in every Sunday.

Now there was April, cosying up to him in the booth he and his late wife had always sat in, and what does that little brat say? 'You look like you're gay. Are you gay?'

Heather turned just in time to see Mr Patel's lip quivering.

'April!' she cried, storming to the table so fast she nearly bowled the girl over. She couldn't remember the last time she'd felt so angry. Her arms were actually quivering with ire. 'Get out of my sight this minute. I've had it with you!'

April's expression fell, though only momentarily. She recovered fast, and beamed a clever little smile. 'What? I never said there was anything wrong with being gay. Me, I'm bisexual.'

'I don't care.' Heather wasn't screaming. Her voice wasn't even loud. It was deep, reverberating through her body like a bass line. 'I don't care if you're the Queen of Sheba, I want you out of my dining room and away from my customers. Now.'

Though she was blind with rage at April's behaviour, Heather managed to console poor Mr Patel while Rick and some of the other staff stepped up service. 'I'm so sorry,' she just kept telling him. 'Rick will fire her, I promise. I am so, so sorry.'

If there was one thing Heather hated, it was apologising for staff's behaviour, especially when it wasn't her hire.

The day went on far too long, with April sneaking back onto the front lines, claiming she just wanted to help. Every damn time she set foot before a customer, the shit hit the fan all over again and Heather had to clean it up.

'Rick, get rid of her!' Heather begged. 'Just pick her up and toss her out the door!'

But Rick hemmed and hawed, claiming he wanted to get to the bottom of the situation before taking extreme measures. He wasn't one for watching disgruntled employees walk out the door. Who knows what they'd come back with?

At closing time, Heather would have killed for a big drink, but there was still cash to be reconciled and the day's deposit to sort out. She always helped Rick with the reconciliation – it gave him an excuse to drive her home.

'Can I have a ride, too?' April asked, poking her head in the office.

Heather said no in conjunction with Rick's, 'Sure, no problem.' He didn't even notice the death glare she shot him. Sometimes that man could be totally oblivious, and it irked Heather despite her attraction to him.

'Want me to help with this?' April swooped in and picked up the pile of debit receipts in one hand and credit-card receipts in the other. Before Heather could shout, 'Put those down!' April had scrambled the piles absently, like she wasn't paying attention to what she was doing. Did she know? Did she realise how much extra work she'd just created for Heather and Rick?

That was it, all Heather could take. She stormed from the office and threw herself into one of the back booths, where she let her head fall into the cradle of her arms. She didn't want to exist right now, just hide inside of herself, inside this empty restaurant. Everyone else had gone home – everyone but herself and Rick ... and goddamn April.

God only knows how long she stayed there, head down in the booth, just waiting for everything to resolve itself somehow. She wasn't quite sure whether she wanted to cry or scream until she felt a long fingernail poking her shoulder.

It was April ... April ... April!

'What?' Heather shrieked, sitting up and pounding her fists against the table. She'd never heard her voice so high-pitched, breaking like glass. 'What do you want now, April? Haven't you tortured me enough?'

That's when she noticed the metal flipper in April's hand. The kitchen staff used those flippers for just about everything done on the grill, and this one was still dripping with fat.

April looked down at her with puppy-dog eyes, begging

forgiveness. 'I'm sorry, Heather. I'll do better on my next shift, I promise.'

'Your next shift?' Heather was in disbelief at this girl's outrageous assumption. 'There isn't going to be a next shift for you, pumpkin.'

April turned from apologetic to just plain bratty. Her expression was like a child's, and when she said, 'Rick said I can,' Heather could have sworn she was about to call him Daddy.

No way this girl would ever win in a game of wills. Heather said, 'Well, I'll have a talk with Rick and clear things up because, honey, it's you or me.'

Waving the metal flipper from side to side, April said, 'It's already settled. Rick said you get to punish me for all the bad stuff I did today.' She set the greasy flipper in the middle of the table, bending over so her butt stuck up in the air.

Heather didn't move. She felt overcome by that haze she woke up in every morning, wondering 'Am I still dreaming or is this real?' But she had a sneaking suspicion this was real, and that it was … well, it was just weird.

'Rick!' Heather called. 'Come out here a sec?'

He jogged from the office and stopped short when he reached the dining room. The stunned look on his face when he spotted April like that told Heather he had nothing to do with this. There she was, leaning down, elbows on the table, hands on either side of the flipper, ass up in the air, and Rick seemed just as shocked as Heather was.

And then a smirk bled across Rick's lips, and he took a step forwards. 'What's ... uhh ... what's going on here?' His tone was incredulous, but sparkling with play.

'You said I could try another shift if I let Heather punish me,' April said simply, like she couldn't understand why they were so confused. 'So I found this greasy thingy in the kitchen, and I thought ...' Her eyes went wide for a moment, like she was puzzling over the situation too. 'Or did you want her to spank me with her hand?'

'Spank you?' Rick took a few steps back. 'Are you playing with us, April? Is this some kind of joke?'

Shaking her head, April replied, 'No, sir. I never joke about spankings.' She chuckled, and her freckled cheeks flushed. 'I like them too much to tease.'

Heather had been watching Rick all this time, but now she turned her attention to April's bratty little grin. 'Did you annoy us deliberately so we would spank you?'

Never in a million years would Heather have imagined that sequence of words crossing her lips.

April didn't respond, except to giggle, and that raised Heather's temperature another few degrees.

'What good will it do?' Heather asked, wanting a real answer, something she could tell herself to justify the action she was about to take. She rose awkwardly from the booth, scooped up the flipper and stood behind April.

'It won't bring back the customers you've alienated. It won't un-hurt the people you offended. So what good will it do?'

Flipping her modest black skirt up over her ass, April turned her head and replied, 'It'll make you feel a hell of a lot better – that's a guarantee.'

Heather couldn't maintain a lock on April's gaze. She was too enraptured by the sight of that round ass. It was damn near perfect, its surface only disrupted by the odd freckle, and pretty much unhindered by April's thong: red lace with a little satin floret set into the band, right in the middle. Heather was getting all warm between the legs. As she gripped the handle of her makeshift paddle, she realised the crotch of her panties was rather wet, too. How could she possibly have gone from incensed to aroused this quickly?

'Should I do it?' Heather asked Rick.

He shrugged one shoulder, fixating on April's ass. 'You don't need my permission.'

That caught in Heather's chest, and she looked at him hard. 'I don't?'

He must have seen in her eyes how eagerly she wanted to be his, to belong to him, because he shook his head and nodded to April, like he didn't want to admit their relationship in front of her.

'Please,' April begged. Her voice was small and strained, like she couldn't bear another moment's wait.

'I was sooo annoying today. I deserve it sooooooo much!'

'That's true,' Heather reasoned. She nearly smacked the flipper against her own hand before remembering how greasy it was. 'OK, well ...' She looked quickly to Rick, and then back to April's nice round butt. 'I guess I'm doing this, then.'

'How many?' April asked.

Heather could almost feel the girl's pussy muscles contracting as those mountainous cheeks tightened. 'I don't know ... ten?' She'd never doled out this kind of punishment before.

'How about ten each?' April begged, looking now to Rick. 'Pretty please? I've been so bad!'

'Yes,' Heather hissed without waiting for Rick's response. In fact, she couldn't wait for anything any more. She had to start this now!

Stepping to the side, closer to Rick, Heather slapped the flipper against April's ass, leaving a greasy splotch in her wake. She'd only struck one cheek, but both jiggled, and the motion mesmerised Heather.

Rick's heat sizzled against Heather's backside as she geared up for another go. She did two this time, both on the other cheek, and revelled in the sound of April's pleasured pain. It was a hiss each time, after the fourth and the fifth, too. It was a smacking sound, a little wet from the grease, a little slippery and messy, and then

April's quickly indrawn breath. The girl whimpered, and that noise in particular made Heather feel vindicated.

She'd doled out half her spankings already. They were going by too fast. Should she hand over the baton now, or keep at it?

'How does that feel?' Heather asked. And then there were six. She couldn't restrain herself. 'Does it hurt? Does it sizzle?'

'Harder,' April groaned. Her voice was so low it sounded like it was coming from her belly, a desperate plea.

So Heather went harder. Maybe she'd been a touch hesitant before, but not any more. Now she whacked April's ass, letting the metal bounce and rebound before going in for another, and yet another. What was that? Seven, eight, nine. Only one more to go. Better make it good.

'Where do you want it?' Heather asked. The left cheek was redder than the right, but the right had more grease gleaming off the skin.

'Anywhere!' April cried. She sounded like she was choking on the words, so desperate, so desirous of painful pleasure.

Heather swung back, stepping on Rick's foot and not even apologising before whacking April's ass with all her strength. Both cheeks were still rippling and recoiling when Rick took the flipper from her hand, urging her out of the way. He started in without hesitation, and his very first spank sent April bouncing against the table.

'Owww!' she screeched.

Heather was impressed, but she also felt a little useless. She hadn't inspired anything near that reaction.

'Again!' April whimpered, turning around like she was searching for sensation in tangible things. 'Do it again!'

Rick tossed the flipper from one hand to the other, and then back. 'You sure you can take any more? Your butt is looking pretty pink.'

It was true. Heather hadn't noticed before, but April's ass was rosy red ... and greasy to boot. She hovered over April's body, close by, feeling the heat coming off her like an oven. She watched from above as Rick brought the flipper down on April's ass for a second, third, fourth time. Those sounds, the slap, slap, slap of lubricated metal on flesh, made Heather's pussy spasm and clench. God, the way that girl's cheeks undulated when they got spanked probably turned Heather on as much as it did April.

'You were a bad girl today,' Rick growled. The gravel in Rick's voice did it for Heather, and for a second she wondered if she should feel jealous, but she was just too caught up in the moment.

Heather unzipped her black slacks and pushed them down to the floor. She scrambled out of her shoes, socks, underwear, leaving it all in a pile. Her fingers flew to her shirt buttons as she climbed up on the bench seat. When she got up on the table wearing only a pink lace bra and knelt in front of April's face, the bratty girl wore an expectant grin.

'Eat me, you little monster.' Heather held open her pussy lips right in front of April's mouth, so close she could feel the girl's laboured breath rustling her trim pubic hair.

'Heather!' Rick cried. His eyes opened wide and his jaw set askew as he gawped at her nearly naked pose. 'What are you doing?'

'She's been bad,' Heather replied. 'You said so yourself, and ten little spanks just didn't do it for me.' She gazed down into April's taunting eyes and said, 'But this will.'

April extended her velvet-pink tongue and Heather shifted closer until her clit was pressed right up against it. The moment their hottest and wettest parts touched, a sizzle of liquid pleasure shot through Heather's chest. Her heart beat wildly as April arched her head up to lick, lick, slowly lick, and then plant her whole mouth over Heather's mound and suck.

Heather arched so violently that she nearly pulled her tender clit out of April's mouth. God, she could have done a back flip, the sweet pleasure was so intense. Her body wanted to rock, wanted to writhe against April's mouth, but she was too afraid of popping her clit out of that deep wet hold.

'Rick,' Heather pleaded, her voice thin as silk. 'Rick, spank her. Spank her!'

Smack – that was five for Rick.

The ripple of April's flesh, the way the girl moaned, 'Mmmm,' arching her back and begging with her butt, made Heather crazy with lust. Grinding her pussy against April's mouth, she rode the girl's tongue, losing suction but gaining something altogether grittier.

Rick edged back from April's rocking ass and shook his head. 'I've had it with this thing,' he said, tossing the flipper onto the vinyl bench seat. It slid all the way to the end but, before it had even come to a rest near the wall, Rick's bare hand fell hard against April's ass.

'Oh, God!' she squealed, writhing upon the table, making Heather squirm above her, trying to regain alignment with that pleasure-hungry mouth. 'Give me another one.'

And Rick did, a seventh spank, the second with his bare palm. April squealed differently in reaction to Rick's hand than she had to the metal, and Heather tried not to feel envious that the man she loved was making skin-to-skin contact with this annoying young woman. After all, Heather's most intimate flesh was grinding against April's tongue. There was nothing like the full oral treatment, and Heather squirmed and shifted to squeeze every delight she could from that mouth.

Behind April's glowing pink ass, Rick let the flat of

his hand spank her so hard and fast Heather could have sworn she heard him sweeping the air out of his path.

When Rick's hand fell against April's hot flesh, Heather was sure she felt the sensation too. It actually ... hurt! And not just April, but Rick as well. She could hear it in the hissing sounds they shared, and see it in the wincing expressions on their faces. But, despite the hurt, Rick launched at April again, his firm hand falling on her rosy cheek. That one didn't seem to smart quite as much, so he wound up for another and let his palm smack April's greasy cheek hard, again and again. God, the way that flesh jiggled, rippling, writhing, undulating from the force of that spanking, made Heather so excited she bucked heavily against April's face.

More! Oh, she wanted more, so much more! But when Rick wound up for another blow, April jerked back to block her cheeks with both hands. 'That's it,' she said. 'You've hit your ten. No more spankings.'

Heather gasped for breath. April did, too, face planted between Heather's thighs, chest rising and falling as quickly as she licked at Heather's pussy. Heather's muscles twitched, her arms especially. She wasn't finished with this girl. She had so much more inside of her, so much more to give.

April's ass glowed red, so bright Heather had trouble turning her gaze from those pretty pink cheeks to the girl's dark eyes.

'I was so bad,' April said, her gaze dull with blatant desire. 'I won't be bad again … not here …' God, she was pleading, just pleading with Heather, her chin dripping with pussy juice. 'I'll be good here, if you keep me.'

Heather's head was buzzing. This couldn't end. She didn't want it to end.

'Rick's going to fuck you now,' Heather said, raising her eyes to him, granting him permission. 'Rick's going to fuck you so hard you won't be able to sit for a week.'

He wasted no time unbuckling his belt and dropping his pants around his ankles. His cock sprang free like a jack-in-the-box. It led the rest of his body between April's thighs. When he shifted the girl's red thong to one side, Heather only wished she could see just how wet and swollen April's pussy had become through all the spankings.

Gripping the girl's gleaming ass with one hand, Rick wrapped the other around his erection and aimed it between April's legs. Heather couldn't see, but she knew when his cockhead had burst into April's pussy by the girl's blissful gasp. Pressing both hands down on the girl's rosy ass, Rick began to rock in her, making her whole body shift against Heather's.

They were quiet, all three of them, while Rick fucked April. Her breath fell hot against Heather's throbbing clit. For an eternal moment, that was enough.

But when that moment ended, Heather smashed her

pussy into April's mouth and growled, 'Suck it. Make me come.'

'Uh-huh!' April agreed while Rick moaned behind her. She suctioned Heather's clit between her blazing lips. 'Mmm!'

April sucked so hard Heather wondered if she might be growing a huge dick inside the girl's mouth. That's what it felt like. She thrust her pelvis forward, rocking against April's face, watching as the girl scrunched up her brow and hummed around Heather's clit. It felt so good, so good beyond good, that Heather knew she wouldn't last long.

She also knew exactly what would put her over the edge.

Tearing into the cups of her bra, Heather pulled out her tits and pressed them together. When she caught Rick watching her, she smiled and he said, 'Oh, you're gonna make me blow, looking at those things.'

With a sly smile, Heather pinched her nipples, sending a jolt of electricity through her body. Her clit buzzed inside April's hot mouth, and she bucked and writhed, chasing that orgasm in tight circles and finding it against April's tongue.

'Oh fuck,' Rick moaned as Heather kept on torturing her tits. 'Fuck, I'm gonna come.'

He pulled his cock from April's pussy and it gleamed with her juices. Heather watched as he stroked it so fast his hand was a blur. April turned to watch, but Heather caught her head with both hands and shoved it back between her legs, summoning yet another orgasm with the girl's hot mouth.

Rick's throat clicked and he made that familiar noise, something between a choke and a yelp. A blast of come streamed from his dick, landing like a white rope on April's rosy ass. Her skin was so greasy Rick's jizz slid towards her crack. She moaned around Heather's throbbing clit, wiggling as spurt after spurt of Rick's come erupted against her flesh.

Heather's body glistened with a slick sheen of sweat as she pulled herself away from April's mouth. Despite all the rutting good sex she and Rick had been at all weekend, she couldn't remember the last time she had felt quite this depleted. She wanted to slip down from the table and fetch herself a drink, but she knew her legs wouldn't support her.

'April?' Heather asked, eyeing the bar. 'Would you pour me a nice chardonnay? I'm absolutely spent.'

Heather rolled down from the table in time with April, and stretched out on the bench. She could almost taste the wine on her tongue, and that made her think about how April's mouth must taste of pussy.

Rick set himself in the bench seat across from Heather, and his hazy smile spoke volumes. They gazed at each other worshipfully, an unbreakable bond – until a crash rang out from the bar.

April had dropped Heather's glass and it had shattered, sending chardonnay splashing across the floor. The girl looked from the mess to Rick to Heather, her eyes wide. 'Oops. Sorry. My hands were greasy, I guess.'

Reaching for Rick's equally greasy hand, Heather grasped it and squeezed. They watched April pick up glass shards and fetch the mop, doing these chores bare-assed and ineffectively.

When the floor was relatively clean, Heather shook her head and laughed. 'Come on, April, it's time to go home – all three of us. We'll punish you there for breaking that glass later on.'

Smiling but silent, April arranged her skirt, tucking her white top into it, wiggling her hips, biting her lip. She took off, skipping towards the door, and a thrill scintillated through Heather's body, from her fingers to her toes and everywhere in between.

For His Pleasure
Valerie Grey

I got a job at an academic publisher where my art history degree was actually beneficial: I managed the various art criticism and literary journals (sending out manuscripts to peer reviewers and editors, then keeping track of the production for those articles accepted for publication) and acquired textbooks in art, mathematics and social sciences. The firm was taken over and we all thought we were going to lose our jobs, but it wasn't that bad. Some people had to go, but I had been there quite a long time and I was staying.

The only change was that we got a new executive managing editor from the company that took us over. He was a rough-looking brute with a Scottish accent. He introduced himself and told everybody he wanted a happy workforce, but he was frightening. He was forty-four and very tall, which I am not (I am five feet two), and he had a loud, forceful and commanding voice.

Twice during the first week he came to me and said I had done a lousy job copy-editing some manuscripts. The first time he threw two manuscripts down in front of me on my desk and yelled.

'This isn't good enough, Ms Sheraton! Look at these! Three errors in grammar and one misspelled word. We are a professional company here. We publish important and verified articles and books. We cannot afford to look like amateurs.'

I couldn't look up at him. I just mumbled, 'Sorry' and left the office.

Next time it happened there were three manuscripts with one error in each. He threw them down on my desk again.

'You should know how to handle copy-editing and production properly by now, Ms Sheraton!'

I think he sensed something about me that interested him because the next thing he said was that if I valued my job I was going to have to get my head out of the clouds and concentrate better; yet his voice was softer than usual.

At the end of the week we were having a big meeting. All the new top bosses were going to be telling us about their plans for the company and what had to be done for us to survive in the new situation.

120

As we were moved to the meeting, one of the managers, Montgomery, shook a manuscript at me. 'We can't have any more of these poor standards. That deserves six of the best, I think. Don't you, Christine?'

I was surprised he addressed me by my first name. Before I could say or do anything he stomped off to the meeting. The management said a load of stuff that I didn't really understand except that things were going to be tough and we all had to work harder and better for no more money. Drinks and sandwiches were laid on afterwards and I had had a couple more glasses of vodka than I ought to when Montgomery came over to me.

'You and I need to talk. Come on out to my car, Christine.'

Before I knew what I was doing I was following him out to the car park. Soon we were driving along in a direction that I didn't know and my head was spinning. I didn't dare say a word and I was scared.

Montgomery drove into really dark woodland and then into a picnic place. There was nobody around at all. He got out of the car, came round to my side and opened the door.

'Get out.'

Still without saying anything I did what he said. He took my arm and led me round to the front of the car. It was a big black Volvo with a long front. He told me to bend over and put my hands on the bonnet. I wasn't sure whether to do what he said or not, but I did.

'You know your work isn't up to standard, don't you, Christine?'

I didn't really want to agree, but I heard myself saying, 'Yes ...'

'Yes, Sir. And it will always be Sir in future in this sort of situation. Do you understand?'

'Yes, Sir.'

'You have got to make your mind up now. There are two choices. Either I put you on a warning and you start down the route of losing your job, or you agree that I help you improve your standards. Which is it to be?'

'I don't understand. How –'

'Sir! Get back in the car and I will give you a warning in the Personnel Office on Monday.'

'Oh! No, Sir. Please help me, Sir.'

'Are you sure?'

'Yes, Sir. Please help me. I can't lose my job.'

'This is the deal. You get six of the best on your bottom now with my belt. At the end of every week I will review your progress and see what correction you might need. Do you understand?'

My panties were soaked. I was still frightened, but I was excited too. I had felt this feeling before, in college, when I had let two men do certain sexual things to me.

'I understand, Sir.'

'I am going to spank you with my belt and you shall agree. After each stroke you call out the number and say, "Thank you, Sir."'

I heard him undo his belt. Nothing happened for a few seconds and then there was a hard whack on my bottom. It really hurt. I yelped a little bit and forgot that I had to call out the number.

'We will start again. This one is still going to be number one. If you don't call it, well, it doesn't count.'

This time he took hold of the waist of my trousers and pulled them down to my thighs.

He got back in place and very soon I felt the sharp thwack of the leather belt on my buttocks. I yelped again. The pain was sharper this time, but I did remember what I had to do.

'One. Thank you, Sir.'

After the third stroke I had managed to stay in place and count properly, but my bottom was really stinging. Instead of carrying on, Montgomery took hold of my knickers and yanked them down. I was so embarrassed. What if somebody drove in or a dog walker came by? I thought. For all I knew there could be somebody now lurking behind a tree and seeing all this. And then I flushed bright red again. I thought about my wet knickers. Montgomery must have seen that and even felt it. So embarrassing. I didn't have time to wonder or worry any more as the fourth stroke of the belt landed. He was standing on the other side of me now and the end of the belt curled round my other hip.

I was crying. 'Four. Thank you, Sir.'

'Just in time. You nearly got another one then.'

My whole bottom was on fire. 'Five. Thank you, Sir.'

I managed to get back in position and the last stroke hit me straight away. When I had called out the number and I knew it was finished I didn't get up. I wasn't sure what was going to happen next. I was worried about being seen, but I was also starting to feel a really warm, tingling glow. My bottom was hurting, but there was a nice feeling as well and I was more excited than I could ever remember.

'Straighten your clothes and get in the car.'

I did as I was told, wriggling to try to get comfortable on my punished bottom. He didn't say much as we drove. He took me to the end of my street. As I got out of the car he said, 'Work as normal Monday, then Friday I will see what you need. You want to keep your job, don't you?'

* * *

Friday. I wasn't sure what would happen. My work had been pretty good during the week, but instead of wearing my usual trousers I put on a short pleated skirt and a white thong. Montgomery was waiting in his car at the kerb when I walked out of the building.

'Get in.'

I did.

He drove away without saying anything. He parked on in front of an apartment building only a few blocks away from where I lived. We went inside and took the stairs to the third floor. He led me to his flat. It was very smart. From the hall I could see a kitchen/diner and then a living room next to it, but he took my arm and drew me to a bedroom door.

'Decision time again. If you go in this room you leave your clothes and your name outside. In there you are my property just like my bed. You do exactly what I tell you to do without question. You can leave the flat any time you want, but if you leave when I am not ready for you to go, well, slut, you never come back. Do you want to go in?'

I didn't answer. I looked at the floor.

'Off you go home. I'll be looking carefully at your work next week. You know that, don't you?'

I quickly said, 'No. Please, Sir, I want to go in. Please!'

'Are you certain?'

'Yes, Sir. Please.'

'Take your clothes off and drop them down there. As I said, you are not Christine Sheraton in there. You are the thing I use. If I want your mouth I will say "mouth" and you will open it for me to use. The same goes for any other part of you.'

I dropped my clothes on the floor and he pushed me through the door. It was a nice big bedroom with a king-size bed and a shower room and toilet in one corner. What I saw straightaway though was a great big window that Montgomery was pushing me towards. Right in front of the window he told me to put my hands behind my head and spread my legs apart. We were a long way up, but I was sure that people must be able to see me. I didn't dare look down. I fixed my eyes on the sky.

Montgomery moved some things around on the bed behind me and then he came round in front. He had a riding crop in his hand. You know, the things that jockeys use to make their horses run faster. He couldn't really be going to hit me with that, could he? It obviously hurt a racehorse.

He tapped me lightly under the chin with the leather flap at the end of the crop.

'Shoulders back, tits out. They're not very big. Make the most of them for your admirers. Maybe in one or two of the boats out there a couple of guys have their binoculars in your direction.' He slid the crop down and jiggled one of my breasts with it. 'We'll give them some attention another time.' He carried on down. 'This bush has got to go. I told you. No clothes in here. My cunt must be properly displayed. You will have it shaved absolutely clean when you come next time. Not the tiniest bristle.

'Understand?'

'Yes, Sir.'

He told me to get face-down on the bed. I turned and saw he had piled four pillows in the middle. It was obvious what I was supposed to do. I climbed over the pillows and lay with my bottom sticking up high on top of them. His headboard had round wooden things in it like chair legs and he told me to hold on to them.

'Six again today. Not with that nice soft belt, but with my trusty crop here. Remember what you have to do?'

The next thing I knew was a whistling and a terrible pain in my bum just as I heard the 'crack' sound on my skin. I bounced on the pillows. I really didn't want to make a noise. That was partly because I thought there must be another flat on the other side of the bedroom wall. I just about managed to keep quiet.

'One. Thank you, Sir.'

Montgomery walked round to the other side of the bed and almost before I could think I heard that whistle. A little squeal escaped from my mouth and then I managed to get myself together. 'Two. Thank you, Sir.'

He moved back to the other side before giving me the third stroke. As I managed to say the count, with a tremble I started worrying that I was making his bed wet with tears and dribble. With the fourth crack on my bum I screamed properly and I suddenly realised that I was leaking pussy juice onto his pillows. I could feel that I was streaming.

I didn't have to worry about that for long. As soon as I managed to stumble through the count of four he told me to get onto my back and he threw the pillows on the floor. I was confused. I knew I had to have six. I was wondering how I could take it because my bottom was throbbing, but surely he wasn't going to let me off two.

'Grab your ankles and hold them as wide apart as you can.'

My ass was still stinging like mad and I hoped that this new angle might mean that he would hit a spot that hadn't already been punished. Nothing could have prepared me for what did happen.

'Carry on with the count from four.'

I saw him raise his arm and heard the swish as the crop came down. He hit me right between my legs and I yelled out loud, letting go of my ankles, then grabbing them again as quickly as I could and remembering the count.

'Five. Thank you, Sir.'

He raised his arm again.

My pussy lips were on fire after that last stroke of the crop and I only just managed to say the count. I let go of my ankles and clasped both hands between my legs trying to hold down the pain. Just as I was beginning to wipe away my tears and, like before, beginning to feel that warm tingly glow along with the pain, he told me to get off the bed and onto my knees with my hands clasped behind my back.

'You are going to have to have that hair off in future to show it off properly.

'Now. You have been saying thank you. It is time to learn how to give proper thanks for your training.'

He undid his zipper and I opened my mouth. He put his cock in my mouth and told me how he wanted it licked and sucked. While he was doing this he held me by my hair and moved my head how he wanted it. He said that I had to learn how to take him right into my throat and when he was ready to come I had to collect it on my tongue to show him. He told me to relax and he pulled my head really hard towards him. I felt the head of his dick at my throat and he said 'Swallow.' I tried, but just gagged and coughed. He slapped my breast and pushed his prick in my mouth again. He tried another three or four times. I gagged every time, but it did go a way down my throat once.

'I am going to come. Make sure you don't spill any or you will be punished.'

He shot a really big load of sticky come into my mouth. I was surprised that it was so much, but I did manage to keep it all in. He told me to look up and open my mouth. He stood aside so that I could see myself in the wardrobe mirror door. There was a big pool of white come nearly filling my mouth.

'Swallow.'

He told me that was it for today and to make sure I was properly prepared for next week when there would be new developments. I put on my clothes outside the bedroom, but he wouldn't let me have my thong back. He told me to fold my skirt waist over twice so that it was ridiculously short. He led me to the lift and told me to walk home.

* * *

During the week I made two or three mistakes at work. All I got from Montgomery was a kind of scowl and I imagined him clocking up a list of offences in his head that he would correct later. On Friday I went to work in the short pleated skirt instead of my usual trousers. After hesitating a few times and worrying about it I finally set off with no knickers on. I put a thong in my handbag, just in case.

All day I had problems whenever I had to reach for anything in case I was showing a bare ass. It was almost a relief when it was time to go home although I was anxious about what would happen next. I looked out for Montgomery as I made my way slowly to the door. Suddenly he was at my side. Instead of taking me with him he just said, 'My flat, nine p.m.'

* * *

130

My knees were trembling when I rang the doorbell. Montgomery opened the door.

'Go to the bedroom.'

I quickly took off my clothes and opened the bedroom door. When I saw the two naked men with hoods on their heads I screamed with shock.

'Shut up. Kneel and welcome your hosts properly.'

I dropped to my knees. Montgomery grabbed my hair and pushed my face into a strange crotch. Stiff, greying pubic hairs tickled my face before the soft prick starting to stir brought my attention back to what I was obviously expected to do. I opened my mouth, slipped it in and felt it grow quickly in response to my sucking and licking.

The prick quickly became very hard and filled my mouth, then Montgomery dragged my head away and pushed my face into the next groin. When I had brought that prick to a stiff erection he pulled me away again and plugged his own semi-hard prick into my slobbering mouth. As he was pumping into my throat Montgomery said that I had just met some of the senior management of the new company and I was going to be introduced to others in the future.

He told me that I had a special task to carry out. I would be marked on my performance in the most appropriate way. That is, marked on my body with his cane for any failure to provide the highest quality work.

Taking his prick out of my mouth I had the first opportunity to get a proper look at the men, above waist level. They were both older men. One had a large paunch, a beer belly perhaps, and the other was very skinny. I couldn't tell much else about them except the skinny guy had very distinctive blue eyes shining through round holes in his hood. It was scary enough to be offered to strangers for their use, but their wearing hoods made it even more menacing.

'Please prepare to be serviced, gentlemen.'

They both knelt with their backs to me and with their elbows on the carpet.

'Suck him.'

Montgomery pointed to beer belly. He walked the short distance to me and put his soft dick in my mouth. It was some relief to have the different movement. I had him hard very soon. Obviously I was made to do the same for skinny and Montgomery, but then there was no break before the second round of ass licking. This must have been the longest fifteen minutes of my life. Twice Montgomery said I wasn't doing the job properly and added two cane strokes each time.

I sank on my knees, massaging my jaw as best I could with my hands. I was worrying about the caning that I was going to get, but that wasn't going to happen yet. Montgomery said, 'Suck him' once again and I had no chance to think or move before beer belly grabbed my head and pulled me onto him. He was hard quite quickly, but it didn't end there this time. He was fucking my face quite hard. Before long he was thrusting into my throat and then he was mumbling.

He shot his load into my mouth. Montgomery told me to show it to them all and then I was made to swallow it. Skinny was already as stiff as a tent pole. He eagerly thrust into my sticky mouth. His prick was longer. I gagged several times as he fucked my throat. He was pressing his hand to the front of my neck so he could feel his prick go in and out of my throat. He didn't come as quickly as the first man. Slowly I got used to the action and realised that my face was not as cramped any more. When he did shoot his load I knew that I had to keep it in my mouth to show them before swallowing it and moving on to service Montgomery.

A couple of weeks ago I could never have imagined this. I had just been used for sex by complete strangers, doing things that I would have said were disgusting. Now I was being face-fucked by a man who had beaten me and was going to do it even more. Instead of being outraged, I knew that my pussy was sopping wet and I really wanted to please Montgomery. His prick was familiar in my mouth and I worked my aching jaw for all I was worth to try to give him the best experience I could. When he shot his load I had the biggest mouthful of the evening. I showed it round proudly to the other men while I waited for the order to swallow.

'Thank you for your assistance in this training session, gentlemen. Enjoy the rest of your evening.'

Montgomery showed the two guys out of the bedroom. Presumably they dressed and left.

He turned back from the bedroom door and thrust his fingers into my soaking cunt, then slid his hand up my pubic bone.

'Very smooth. Kneel.'

I felt a little disappointed that he hadn't commented on how my pussy looked. It had startled me when I followed Montgomery's instructions and removed my rather luxuriant pubic hair. Seeing the cleft of my cunt lips for the first time as an adult was very odd. It certainly made me look more naked.

'You earned six strokes of the cane today for your lack of commitment and effort. Your slackness at work during this last week requires a further four strokes of my belt. For no reason other than that it pleases me, you will also receive four strokes of the riding crop.'

I couldn't possibly explain why, but I felt a tingle about pleasing him by being whipped. At the same time I was very apprehensive about my beating.

Montgomery took a length of cord from his bedside cabinet and bound my wrists and elbows behind my back. He then tied my ankles to the bed legs so that my feet were about three feet apart with my back to the bed. I was puzzled. I didn't see how I could get my punishment in this position. But he wasn't finished. He now tied my breasts tightly so that they stuck right out.

'You will call out the number of each stroke followed by "Sir". If you fail to number the stroke or you call it incorrectly, it will be repeated.'

After taking a cane from his cabinet he held my wrists firmly in his left hand. There were a couple of aiming taps and then I heard the whistle before the sharp crack on my buttocks that was followed by a horrible pain.

'One, Sir.'

I was sweating. The fierce stinging was awful and then I heard the whistle. I gasped when I heard the crack and the second wave of pain shot through my body. Confused, I took a few seconds to call out.

'Two, Sir.'

'Just in time. Take care.'

He let go of my wrists and moved round in front of me. He ran the cane down my body from my tits to my thighs and back up again. He looked into my eyes and then raised his arm. The cane hit me right in the belly and knocked the wind out of me. I let out a little squeal and bent forward.

'Stand up.'

I did and called the third stroke.

He put the fourth stroke right across the front of my

pussy. Five was on the tops of my thighs and then the final one was back on my belly. Tears were streaming down my face now and I couldn't help yelling as each stroke landed. It was as much as I could do to keep calling the numbers, but I did manage it. Montgomery returned to the cabinet, carefully put away the cane and returned with the riding crop.

'How many will you receive from this?'

'Four, Sir.'

'And why are you getting them?'

'For your pleasure, Sir.'

'Right. Don't forget to count. You start at the beginning again. My pleasure is counted separately.'

'Yes, Sir.'

Standing in front of me, Montgomery lined up the crop on my right tit. It was purple now because of the cord tied round it. My head was swimming. I hadn't thought of this. Could I stand it?

There was not much time to think about it. The thwack of the crop resounded. I looked down to see the bright welt caused by the leather flap at the end of the crop.

'One, Sir.'

The next one was on the same spot on the other breast. As soon as I called out the number, he took me by the shoulders and laid me back on the bed. He stood above me with one foot on either side of my head, and lined up the crop again. This time he brought it down on the

136

underside of my right breast and followed that very soon with the final pleasure stroke. Once I had numbered the fourth cropping, Montgomery knelt down so his ass was on my face. He ran his hands over my burning tits. I got my tongue into his ass as best I could.

'Start counting from one.'

Montgomery raised the belt over his shoulder. I couldn't see what was happening; the slap of the leather against my wet pussy lips made my ass leap from the bed and I screamed. I had never felt anything like it.

Such pain in my cunt, but the places where the cane and the crop had landed earlier were now starting to tingle in a way that wasn't bad. There was a sort of warm glow there.

'Too late. Start again from one.'

A wet splat and my twat was on fire.

'One, Sir,' I called out. No scream this time. My concentration was totally on getting the numbers right

I managed to keep the count for the remaining three. When he had finished, Montgomery shoved the wet belt against my nose before wiping it dry on my stinging tits.

'Slut.'

He untied my ankles, turned me over and released my arms.

'Get dressed and walk home.'

I left the bedroom and put my clothes on. My legs

were trembling. It was hard to walk properly because of my sore cunny, but the pain was subsiding.

Struggling to fasten my blouse over my burning tits, I thought how nicely they had been tortured for his pleasure.

And for mine.

Eye of the Beholder
Kathleen Tudor

Sandra entered a last few transactions into the spread-sheet, and saved it with a sigh. She was good at book-keeping, but that didn't mean she had to like it, especially when she had a client like Rick, who refused to use online banking and insisted on mailing her every paper receipt.

'Is everything all right?' Gabriel asked from behind her. She felt his voice tease the shivers out over the back of her neck, and straightened.

'Yes, sir, just finishing up my last account for today. He's a pain in the ass, but he never pays me late,' she said, smiling. 'I was thinking about getting a head start on tomorrow.'

'Nonsense. If you're finished for today, then you deserve to relax.' His hand went lightly up her arm and across the back of her neck, and she shivered in anticipation even as dread crept into the pit of her stomach.

'Really, I'm fine. The Baker account always takes for ever, so I should probably just start sorting out –'

'Sandra.' He didn't raise his voice to cut off her babbling, just spoke her name in his calm, even tone. She sat stiff and silent before him, her body quivering like a small animal watching a hawk dive in its direction.

She waited for him to speak, knowing he wouldn't appreciate any more of her excuses. He stood patiently, his hand on her shoulder like an anchor. 'Why do you want to avoid being rewarded?' he asked.

'It's just that I'm not in the mood,' she started, but he snorted.

'You're always in the mood. Would you like to try again?'

She'd protested that her stomach hurt, once, and had experienced the humiliation of being dragged to the doctor. If she complained that she thought she had a yeast infection, he would probably find a way to make a game out of treating her himself.

She was out of options, except for the truth. 'I haven't shaved myself in four days. I don't want you to see,' she whispered. She usually kept her pussy carefully shaved, moisturised and even tweezed if she'd missed any spare hairs while shaving, but she'd spent the extra-long weekend camping with her father and brother, where even getting alone to pee in peace was difficult. 'I was going to take care of it tonight, before you could see.'

He softened, but not much. His other hand came down gently on her other shoulder, and he started to knead at her knots, lovingly but firmly massaging her shoulders and neck. 'That doesn't matter to me. Go get ready.'

Sandra felt sick as she stood and moved away from him, heading woodenly from the home office that they shared and into their bedroom. She stripped quickly, taking the time to put each garment away in the proper place – socks in the bin, slacks hung up to wear again, blouse on the hanger for dry cleaning – before she steeled herself to walk down the short hall to the house's third and largest bedroom, which her Master had converted into a magnificent dungeon.

He shut the door behind her and the darkness was complete, since heavy leather curtains blocked the rays of the setting sun. 'Light the candles,' he said from behind her, and she felt that familiar squeeze as all of the hair stood up on the back of her neck like it was reaching for him.

She moved on memory and instinct, crossing the room to the first of the small side tables, where the matches were kept. Once the first candle was lit it was easy to travel around the room to light the others, bringing a warm, inviting glow to the playroom.

'Good girl, now let's get you up on the swing,' he said. It had taken him a lot of years to build and buy all of the equipment and toys he wanted for this dungeon, and the sex swing was one of his pride pieces. The swing had been hung from a huge wooden frame that he'd built himself. It was nearly seven feet tall and four wide, giving plenty of room for any of the activities they might want to perform on it.

Sandra walked towards her favourite toy like it was the gallows, her steps slow and dragging. When she turned and sat, she balanced on the very edge of the swing, sitting upright, legs demurely crossed at the ankles.

'Sandra,' he said, and she nearly started crying when his look forced her back, farther onto the swing. He reached into a cabinet that contained bondage tools and came back with two sets of ankle cuffs, which he used to bind her ankles to the outer edges of the swing. 'That's better,' he said.

She closed her eyes to try to block it out, but the image of her unshaved pussy was projected on the inside of her eyelids the way she thought he must see it, stubbled and imperfect and disgusting. She struggled to pull her knees closed, and he batted them apart and eased two thick fingers into her cunt instead.

She did burst into tears then, and he moved away instantly, sliding his fingers out of her ugly pussy and unfastening her ankles so that he could draw her into his arms. She only cried harder, ashamed, and he picked her up and carried her into their bedroom, where he lay her down on the bed and held her until she was calm enough to speak.

'What happened?' he asked. He sounded completely baffled, and it made her give a little hiccupping sob.

'It's so ugly and I didn't want you to see!' she exclaimed, becoming agitated all over again. He shushed her gently and waited.

'What's ugly?'

'My pussy. The hairs are growing and it's so disgusting and gross,' she said.

'Do you think I'm disgusting when my beard grows?' he asked, sounding amused.

'It's not the same!' She sniffled and rolled over, presenting her back to him. It was a risky move, but she was sure he didn't understand. How could he, when he was Master, so beautiful and perfect?

'I need time to think about this,' he said at last. 'You obviously need to be taught a lesson, and I need to decide how best to teach it. Listen closely. You will not harm a single hair on that pussy until I say so. You will not shave them, pluck them, cut them or find any other way to remove your hair. Do you understand me?'

She turned to him, her face ashen with horror. He couldn't possibly mean what he had just said! But he waited, eyebrows raised, until she uttered a quiet 'Yes, Master.'

'Good. Now that that's settled, you are still expected to serve me properly.' He kissed her, and she moved beneath him, knowing what he needed. When he speared her on his cock it was like a benediction.

She moved cautiously through the next few days, gladly giving him sex when he wanted it and trying not to think about her pussy, which was growing hairier and wilder with every passing day. She sometimes found herself sitting on the toilet holding her razor and crying, but she obeyed his directions and never so much as touched it to her skin.

She had just stepped out of the shower on the third day, where she'd washed her bristly cunt quickly and disgustedly, when her Master stepped into the bathroom.

'Towel off and then come to the dungeon, Sandra. It's time to learn your lesson.'

Tears pricked her eyes again, and fear settled in her, but she did as she was told. He led her to a chair in the dungeon and put her feet up at hip height on a bench in front of her. He bound her that way, his hands moving gently over her skin as the slither of the ropes made her moan. Her skin prickled in goosebumps, and each soft touch of hand or cotton rope made her breath come faster and her heart pound with arousal.

She loved, more than anything, to be bound, and he made sure to include it in special occasions. He included it in punishments, too, since she also loved to squirm. Her heart sank when she realised which this would be, and she tested her bonds. Her wrists were bound together at her sides, the rope trailing under the seat of the chair to hold them together. Her ankles were tied to each side of the bench, forcing her legs apart far enough that she didn't think she could even get her knees all the way closed. All of the knots were as tight and unreachable as usual. She stifled a sigh.

Gabriel moved away from her for a moment, then returned with a lamp. It had a flexible neck, and he bent it, aiming it directly at her pussy before snapping it on. She flinched as the area was lit up, bright and stark and unavoidable. She stared at it with disgusted fascination, wanting to avert her gaze but mesmerised by the horrible sight. She started to shake when he placed the small freestanding mirror on the bench between her knees. He knelt beside her, his cheek brushing up against hers, and adjusted the mirror so that she could see her pussy reflected perfectly back at her.

'That,' he said, 'is beautiful.'

Sandra started to cry. There was nothing uglier, she thought, than the sight of those dark, wiry hairs poking up through the creamy skin of her pussy. He waited patiently for her, unflinching as she sobbed, and eventually she ran out of tears, though shame still burned through her.

'Who is Master here?' Gabriel asked.

'You are,' she said. Her voice was weak, but her answer was strong, unhesitating. He had introduced her to the world of submission shortly after they had started dating, and she had taken to it as if it was all she had ever known. It made her feel loved, protected and taken care of, and she put her heart and soul into serving him. He was her Master.

'Am I ever wrong?' he asked. She considered a smart-assed reply, and he stooped into her field of vision, scowling before she had even fully decided to say the words. 'Are my commands ever wrong?'

'No, Master,' she said.

'Then look at it. I want you to look right at your pussy and don't look away. Are my opinions ever wrong?'

'No, Master.'

'I say that your pussy is beautiful, just as it is. Do you contradict me?' His voice was firm, unyielding. He'd backed her into a trap, but she couldn't give him the answer he wanted. She stared at her pussy and her eyes teared up, but she couldn't force the words out. A flicker of black startled her, and then a jolt of sharp pain stung her pussy lips. She watched in amazement as the skin reddened. 'Answer me!'

'I can't!' The crop descended in another stinging arc almost before the words had left her lips, and Sandra whimpered as the leather whipped against the sensitive flesh.

'Are your thighs the size you wish them to be?' he asked.

Sandra paused for a second, confused. 'No, Master,' she said. She'd been working on losing the extra weight that seemed determined to cling to her thighs.

'Are they ugly?'

She was tempted to answer yes, just to slow the steady march of his logic towards her illogical hatred of her stubbled pussy, but she knew better. 'No, Master.'

He grabbed the skin of her thigh in a rough pinch as he leaned over her. 'You are not perfect, but you are beautiful. Even unshaved, your pussy is beautiful.'

'Yes, Master,' she said, hissing the words out through the pain. The burning in her thigh seemed to travel directly to her clit, setting it ablaze like a torch. She could hardly think, her mind tuned in to the pleasure and pain he was causing.

'Tell me your pussy is beautiful,' he said, releasing her.

Sandra hesitated, and the crop descended again. This time it stung her swollen clit, which had peeked out from beneath the protective hood of flesh, and she screamed as lightning slashed through her nerves. It was exquisite, sharp pain and fierce pleasure tangling until the sensation resonated throughout her entire body.

'Tell me your pussy is beautiful.'

'It's beautiful!' she gasped, rushing to spill out the words before he could strike her again.

'Say all of the words. Tell me, "My pussy is beautiful."'
He swung the crop through her field of vision.

'My pussy is beautiful!' she shouted without thinking.

'Good. Again.'

She stared at the dark hairs emerging from the soft skin of her pussy and this time the words came out of her as if dragged on a string from deep in her stomach, thick and heavy, choking. 'My pussy is beautiful.'

'Good girl,' he said. She felt that usual stir of warmth at those words, high praise from her Master, the man who had held her safe and comfortable and guided her through her life from the moment he'd collared her. Pleasing him made her feel beautiful and perfect, and her pussy slicked at his purr of approval.

He reached down and ran a finger through the wetness flowing from her body, moving his arm around the mirror so that her view was as unimpeded as possible. He slowly raised his glistening fingers to his lips and licked her honey away. 'Hmm,' he said, 'same delicious taste.' Then he slid two of his fingers into her and started to fuck her with them, slowly, so frustratingly slowly.

'I want to hear you saying it. Don't stop. Tell me over and over,' he purred.

'My pussy is beautiful.' Sandra tried to lift her hips, but the chair started to tip, and she eased back with a whimper as he continued the slow tease. 'My pussy is beautiful. My pussy is beautiful.' It became a desperate chant, a form of begging, and she said it over and over, as she clenched her muscles around his fingers, begging him with her tone, her urgency. 'My pussy is beautiful.' Fuck me! 'My pussy is beautiful!' Please, Master, please make me come!

She felt like she'd been repeating those words – that entreaty – for ever when his fingers finally plunged into her faster, harder. She watched as they vanished inside and emerged, over and over, glistening and strong. His thumb joined the dance, jabbing stiffly over her clit with each thrust, just the way she loved it. The abrasion, the heat, the impact, were the perfect counterpoint to the feeling of his fingers sliding inside, spreading her lips wide and invading her deepest place.

'My pussy is beautiful,' she screamed, trying to hold her eyes obediently on the mirror even as she wanted to throw back her head and let her orgasm claim her completely. 'Oh, God, my pussy is fucking beautiful!' She jerked in her chair and felt it start to tip before his strong hand came down on the wood at her shoulder. Her body twitched and sang, and her eyes hurt as she forced them to stay open and focused, not even daring to blink as the pleasure sent her spiralling out of control.

He didn't remove his fingers from inside her until her spasms had calmed and she sat in relative calm, still staring at her pussy.

'Good girl,' he whispered, smiling up at her. She met

his eyes and smiled back, limp with pleasure and satisfaction, but her Master wasn't done with her yet.

He took something from the nearest table and held it up for her to see. Confusion struck her first, then her eyes went wide and a chill swept over her skin as a cold sweat broke out. 'Now, since you have such a problem with this little bit of hair, let's remove it. You can let me know when you want me to stop, and you can keep the rest.' His grin, she thought, was pure evil.

The first couple of hairs he tweezed hurt, especially since she was so extra sensitive after coming, but she managed to keep her noise to a minimum. After more than a dozen, all clustered in the same small area of her pelvic bone, she squeaked with each sharp twinge. Soon the squeaks and moans ran all together until a single, unending sound of pain and protest flooded from between her lips, but still he continued. When she looked closely, the tiny area he had managed to clear so far was beyond discouraging.

'Stop! Please, Master, stop!'

'You want me to stop?' He yanked another hair out.

'Ah! Yes! Please, stop!'

'You would rather have a hairy pussy?' He plucked two more hairs in quick succession, and she yelped.

'Yes! Please leave the hair!'

He smiled as he stood, tossing the tweezers aside. 'But my dear, I thought you absolutely hated that hair.'

She stared at her pussy, the area over her pubic bone red and puffy where he'd plucked, dark with short hairs where he hadn't reached yet, and started to laugh. It was possibly the ugliest thing she had ever seen, and it was hilarious. Gabriel's lips quirked, but he rocked back on his heels, crossed his arms and waited, while she laughed and laughed until tears spilled down her cheeks.

'I'm sorry!' she gasped. 'Master, I'm sorry!'

'For?' He raised his eyebrows, and that set her off again.

'For laughing!' she said, trying not to choke on the giggles. 'For insulting your property! For not listening! I look ... so ... ridiculous!'

He rolled his eyes and broke his own rules, leaving the room with her still bound to the chair. He returned a moment later with a glass of water, shutting the door firmly behind him. He stood over her giggling form for a moment, then shook his head and tossed the water in her face.

Sandra gasped as the cold water cascaded down her face and breasts and belly, and looked up at him, eyes wide, laughter finally silenced.

'You're forgiven,' he said steadily. She could see the glint in his eye, and she smiled at him, careful to choke back the urge to return to laughter. 'Your pussy,' he said, 'is absolutely beautiful.'

'Yes, Master. Thank you,' she answered.

He smiled and patted her cheek, then he moved the mirror and the light away, and leaned over the bench to bury his face in her cunt. He licked at her juices, moaning in pleasure as he tasted her, and she ground against him as much as she could without knocking herself backwards. Then he bit down hard on her labia, and Sandra moaned. She thought she could feel each of his teeth individually where they bit into her flesh, like a dozen attempts to penetrate her, and she couldn't help but cry out with pleasure.

Gabriel indulged himself, alternating between drinking deeply from her honeyed core and savaging her with his teeth. He reached up with one hand and pinched her nipple roughly, then tugged hard, and the dual sense of sweetness where his tongue lapped over her cunt and sharp pain in her breast made her dizzy with arousal. He slapped down hard on her breast, then began to gently massage it, stroking with his fingers even as he bit down on her clit.

It was more than she could stand. She screamed as the painful orgasm buzzed outward from her clit like an electric current, sending shockwaves through her entire body. His mouth immediately eased on her clit, knowing what she needed, and she moaned gratefully as he drove her gently through the pleasure and out the other side.

'Now then,' he said, waiting until her eyes focused on him before going on, 'you may continue to shave and pluck at this beautiful cunt all you like, but from time to time I will ask you to leave it natural, and we will see if you have taken your new lesson to heart. Do you understand?'

'Yes, Master,' she said, her breath still coming heavily. She thought she might have done so anyway. Perhaps a little stubble wasn't the end of the world.

'Good.' He shifted, untied her legs and helped her lower them gently to the ground as the increased blood-flow to her hips made her hiss in discomfort. 'Now we just have the matter of your punishment to discuss. I forgive you, of course, but you must still be punished for disrespecting my property.' He cupped her mons, his fingers teasing her before he moved to untie her hands.

'I understand, Master.' She shook the discomfort out of her shoulders, noting that while he had released her hands, he had left the ropes tied to her wrists. She was not surprised when he took them and led her by them to a large ring set high on one wall. He threaded the ropes through it and soon had her bound, facing the wall, her arms stretched overhead. She relaxed, putting weight on her wrists and letting it stretch through her back, enjoying the sensation even though she knew what was coming next.

'Ten strokes,' he said. Her back tingled with anticipation as she heard the clink of his belt buckle and the smooth hiss of the leather through the loops. Then the leather crashed down across her back and she cried out, even as the leather whistled through the air for a second stroke. The impact drove her against the wall each time, and the edges of the belt stung as it slammed into her, raising welts.

By the tenth blow she was sobbing, great, heavy gasps that rocked through her entire body, a cleansing and a new start. He released her arms immediately, whispering to her as he caught her before she could fall. He lifted her up and carried her to the swing. She heard his trousers drop to the floor, and this time she spread her legs for him, still crying out every ugly thought as he moved to stand between her legs.

'You're beautiful,' he said. The he shifted his hips and slid into her as easily as breathing, and her tears started to calm as she welcomed him in. 'Go ahead, touch yourself.'

Only an hour before, she would have been horrified by the feel of the short, sharp hairs under her fingers, but her Master had taught her better. She let her fingers slide over the hairs, teasing herself as they sent the signals of imminent contact up her spine. Her Master grabbed her hips and began to thrust, using the swing to fuck her hard and wild, his fingers digging deeply into her flesh.

Sandra increased the pressure of her own touch, leaving her pubic bone behind as her Master and lover slammed his cock home again and again. Her fingers drifted down to feel their bodies where they joined, brushing against his length as he took his pleasure with her. She loved the wet slide of him, the soft flesh, as firm as steel, and the ribs and texture of his veins.

She ground her palm against her clit as she slid her fingers around him, and then it was too much. She shifted urgently, her fingers flying to her clit as she stroked her hard bud in time with his thrusts. Her palms scraped over the rough stubble as she teased herself towards climax, and her entire pussy throbbed with the pleasure that she knew was so close to being released. She squeezed him with her inner muscles, moaning as the pleasure mounted like a red wave behind her eyes.

'My pussy is beautiful,' she gasped, both to please him and because she realised it was true. The look of intensity on his face brightened a little as he smiled ferally at her.

'That's right, baby, it is,' he grunted. 'Now come for me.' And, screaming obediently, pussy pulsing around him, she did.

The Miseducation Of Laura Knill
Elizabeth Coldwell

Laura checks the note again, even though she's looked at it a hundred times since her last essay came back with that bright pink scrap of paper attached to the front page. 'My office. Wednesday 3 p.m.' It's not the first time by any means that she's been asked to see Doctor Bradley to discuss her work in more depth; since she joined his tutor group at the start of her second year here, he's kept a regular check on her progress, concerned that she appears to be falling behind her peers. But he's never asked her to come on a Wednesday afternoon before. And he's certainly never attached such specific conditions to their meeting, conditions she wouldn't dream of discussing with anyone else.

Until today, she's never realised how quiet the

university can fall when there's no one around. No lectures take place on Wednesday afternoons; no research is conducted in the science or psychology blocks. Instead, the whole of the campus is given over to extra-curricular activities, the student body taking the opportunity to let its communal hair down. In the theatre, the drama society is rehearsing their end-of-term production of *The Real Inspector Hound*. Somewhere in the bowels of the union building, the fortnightly newspaper is being laid out: page after page of the same old bitchy student politics no one really wants to read. On the rugby pitch, big men are grappling with each other's thighs and buttocks and calling it sport. And where the neatly manicured lawns give way to a stretch of wild, scrubby woodland, the half-dozen members who comprise the Psychedelic Society are hunting for the mushrooms they believe, when brewed as tea, will expand their collective consciousness and open their eyes to the secrets of the universe.

While student life goes on at its usual, mildly disorganised remove, Laura trots down the corridor, the clack of her Mary Jane shoes unnaturally loud against the scuffed wooden flooring, towards the paternoster that will take her up to Doctor Bradley's room. She'd half expected it to be switched off, but someone must be working elsewhere in the arts building, because the lift continues to makes its usual stately progress, its open stalls, barely big enough to hold two people, moving in

a constant loop. She steps on to the steadily rising platform, leans back against the wall and takes a deep breath.
Part of her still can't believe she's doing this, following
the Doctor's instructions to the letter, but deep down she
knows their relationship has been heading towards this
point since the day she first walked into his tutorial room.

Up, up she travels, past museum sciences, archaeology,
music, English and history of art, till the floor that houses
the modern languages department appears. Laura, as she
still so often does, even after more than a year of using
the thing, slightly mistimes her exit from the paternoster,
so her step down is more of a little hop. Sometimes she's
left it too late, gone a floor too far and had to wait for
an empty stall to take her back where she needs to be.
Unlike some of her friends, she's never had the courage
to ride the lift all the way over the top and down.

At least the door to the secretaries' room is firmly shut,
and the blind pulled down in the universal symbol indi-
cating no one's home. She couldn't bear it if one of those
busybodies bustled past now, looking at her outfit and
judging her. Or maybe they'd realise she must be just
another of the Doctor's girls, and let her pass. From the
way he worded the note, and the whispered rumours that
pass among her fellow students, she can't believe she's the
first to come for a Wednesday afternoon's private tuition.

Though she didn't have to dress quite as sluttily as
she has. If she'd taken a little longer to work on putting

together her outfit, the result might have been very different. But she left it till the last moment, diving into one of the charity shops in the city centre and pulling the first vaguely suitable frock from the rack. Blue and white checks, buttons up the front. Exactly what he'd asked for. Except this dress was cut for someone without half as much in the way of bust and hips as Laura. As a result, it strains across her front where she's fastened it up, and she's had to leave the top couple of buttons undone, showing off rather more than she should of her creamy cleavage. He's also ordered her not to wear a bra, which doesn't improve the effect, as her tits are much too big and heavy to go unsupported for long. Her nipples poke rebelliously at the second-hand cotton; they'd be all too visible if she didn't keep her folder of work clutched tight to her chest.

Teamed with her dress are white over-the-knee socks, the flat, sensible Mary Janes and a jaunty little straw boater. For a School-Disco-style fancy-dress night, she'd be every man's dream: sweet, saucy and, oh, so available. In the cold light of a March afternoon, she can't help but feel a little ridiculous, ashamed of the way her rigid nipples blatantly reveal her excitement, as does the patch of dampness in her white cotton knickers.

Doctor Bradley's door is closed, but she knows he's inside, waiting for her. She knocks and waits for him to call, 'Enter.'

When she does, it's to see him sitting at his desk, reading a sheaf of papers, apparently indifferent to her presence. Her heart seems to flutter up into her throat at the sight of him, as it always does. His hair, more grey than black even though he's barely thirty-five, sticks up where he's been running his hand through it, more than likely in exasperation at something he's read. His tie is askew, and his shirt cuffs are unbuttoned, though he hasn't bothered to roll his sleeves up. When, after a minute or so, he finally looks up to acknowledge her arrival, she's struck by the contrast between the blue of his eyes and his tanned skin. The weather has been unseasonably warm over the weekend, and he's clearly spent time outdoors. She can't help picturing him shirtless in the heat, wondering whether his torso has turned the same appealing shade of light caramel.

'Ah, Miss Knill, there you are.' His deep voice, with its educated Edinburgh twang, cuts into her thoughts. 'Bring your essay to me, then take a seat, would you? There's a good girl.'

She does as he asks, grateful that he hasn't decided to conduct their conversation in French, as he often likes to do. Tense as she is, she doubts she could manage to string a single sentence together.

Unlike his usual tutorial sessions, when four or five students sit grouped in a close semi-circle around his desk, there's only one chair available for her to take. The rest are stacked against the wall, out of the way. Normally Doctor Bradley's study is a scene of mild chaos as everyone struggles to find room in such a crowded space, filled with piles of books and all the clutter he's never quite got round to sorting or discarding. Today, the atmosphere is one of unaccustomed formality. It unnerves and excites her at the same time.

When she sits, the dress gapes open a little way where it stretches across her thighs, and she makes sure to keep her knees tight together. Otherwise, the Doctor would have a clear view up to the stark white triangle of her panty crotch.

Not that he appears to be peeking, his concentration solely on her work. There are two windows in his corner office, looking down on to the gravelled forecourt of the arts building, but she can't see out of them from where she sits. Instead, she gazes over the Doctor's head, concentrating on a row of classic late nineteenth- and early twentieth-century novels, some in French, some in their English translations, fighting for space on the bookshelf behind him.

He takes his time reading her essay, and she tries not to fidget while she waits. Occasionally, he tuts, crossing out a word or scrawling something in the margin with his red ballpoint pen. Once, he even laughs out loud. She can't tell if that's a good sign or not. She's worked hard on the essay, dissecting the breakdown of the marriage between Thérèse Desqueyroux and her husband Bernard with almost forensic detail. When he originally handed it back, he'd asked her to look at some parts of it again and revise them, and she had spent a couple of nights hunched over the desk in her room when she'd rather have been in the union bar with her friends. She'd have completed it sooner, but he told her to write it out in longhand, instead of typing it. She supposes he wanted to prevent her simply copying chunks of text into an online translation service, letting it do the hard work of turning English into French, then pasting the result into her essay. The university does its best to monitor student essays for plagiarism, coming down hard on offenders, but everyone knows there are plenty of ways to cheat the system if you have a mind.

Though Laura wouldn't mind Doctor Bradley coming down hard on her, given the opportunity. But she never cheats where he's concerned, despite the temptation. So many conditions laid down in that little note, and she's obeyed every single one of them. If he wasn't so hot, she wonders, would she have done it? What if ugly old Doctor Jacobs, the head of the department, with his snaggle teeth and his persistent, fishy body odour, had demanded she dress like a schoolgirl from some porno fantasy, and present herself in his office when no one else is around? Would she have objected, reported him to the student welfare service? Thinking about it, she decides probably not. Though it's hard for her to admit, even to herself, that it's what she's being asked to do, as much as the person who's asking her to do it, that turns her on.

'Laura, Laura, Laura …' Doctor Bradley sighs, getting up and coming round his desk to hand her the essay. 'Where do I begin?' Close to him, she can smell the spice of his cologne, mixed with sweat that's as fresh as Doctor Jacobs' is rank. She tries to ignore the nervous flutter of excitement that starts somewhere deep in her core as he bends to point out her many, many mistakes.

'I tried, Doctor Bradley, really I did.'

'I know that.' His tone is not unkind. 'And you've made big strides this term. I'm impressed with how you've finally mastered the past subjunctive tense, and your grasp of nineteenth-century morality is pretty acute. But really, Laura, your handwriting is atrocious. See here –' he points to a word he's circled in red '– I still can't decide whether that's meant to be an "o" or an "e". Not that it matters, because that sentence as it stands doesn't make any sense at all.'

'But you asked me to write it out by hand …' Laura tries not to whine, but this all seems so unfair. She's followed all his instructions to the letter, and yet she still doesn't seem able to please him.

'Indeed I did. And at least you managed to get that right, even if you couldn't find a dress that fits you properly –' The look he gives her, exasperation mixed with unfiltered lust, reminds her that far too much of her cleavage and legs is on display, however decorously she tries to sit, and that her nipples are two tight, unmistakable bumps in the checked fabric. 'Or appreciate the true magnificence of François Mauriac's use of language throughout the novel.'

Something within Laura rebels at last, and she gives vent to her frustration. Hot or not, her tutor can only push her so far, and she's tired of being told that everything she does isn't quite good enough. 'You know what, Doctor Bradley, I really don't care about Mauriac's use of language, or whether it's one of the classics of French literature. I think it's one of the most stupid novels I've ever had to read, boring and pointless, and I wish I'd put that in the essay.'

'Now that I will not tolerate.' There's a sternness to his demeanour that's previously been absent; it startles Laura, makes her wonder what she's let herself in for. 'There's no room in my tutor group for an ungrateful little brat.'

'What – what are you going to do?' She has visions of being handed over to Doctor Jacobs or, worse, Madame Renarde, who's been at the university longer than anyone can remember, and whose teaching style is dry as dust. If that happens, she knows she can kiss goodbye to any chance of hauling up her grades to something even approaching a respectable level.

'I'm afraid there's only one thing I can do, under the circumstances, and that's give you a well-deserved punishment.'

He moves back to his desk, opens the top drawer and removes something. Normally it takes him five minutes to find a fresh pen among all the mess in there, but now he's found exactly what he needs, and she's too busy wondering about that to realise what it is that he's retrieved. Only when he comes back to her does she see he's holding an old black gym shoe, the kind that slips on rather than being laced up, with a thick rubber sole.

'You can't be serious?' Even as she asks, she knows the question is redundant. They're both conducting this bizarre scenario with the utmost seriousness, otherwise why would she have come dressed to fulfil the Doctor's fantasy, and why would he have called her to his room on a Wednesday, when they could just as well have discussed her essay in one of his free periods between lectures?

'Oh, but I am.' His tone brooks no argument, a strange little smile quirking his lips upwards as he approaches her. She can't help taking a quick glance at his crotch, where there's an obvious tenting in his dark-brown corduroy trousers. The bastard's enjoying this – but then, despite whatever she might tell him to the contrary, so is she.

'I'm sorry, Doctor Bradley, really I am.' The stammered

apology, a retraction of her earlier defiance, is the least he can expect even though she knows it won't make a scrap of difference. If she's honest, she doesn't want it to.

'Miss Knill, you have to appreciate that, in this room, what I say goes, and if I decide you're going to bend over my desk so I can spank your bare bottom, that's exactly what you're going to do.' He flexes the plimsoll between his fists, bending it almost in two. Absently, she wonders how many others might have sat here, watching him play with the supple gym shoe, and whether they felt the same rush of heat to their pussy as he outlined the terms of their punishment.

'Spank your bare bottom'. The words seem to burn a sizzling path straight to her sex. The image they create in her brain is scary, but so thrilling it causes her heart to beat in double-quick time. Whatever she expected when she agreed to come here, it wasn't this. To have her panties pulled down for a spanking seems so demeaning, so utterly out of proportion to any defects she might display as Doctor Bradley's student – and yet so right. How could she not have realised it until now?

'Let's not put this off any longer, Laura.' Doctor Bradley puts down the shoe on one corner of the desk and sweeps a pile of papers to one side with his forearm, clearing a space for her. 'Into position, please.'

Laura's hesitancy is not feigned. Even though she wants

this – needs it – with an all-consuming hunger, she's still afraid of feeling that unforgiving plimsoll slapping against her bottom. Her tutor fixes her with a glare. He has picked up the shoe again and is tapping the sole against his palm, letting her know he's waiting. At last she places herself over the desk, feeling the hard edge against her belly, her breasts pancaking against the polished wood. A white china mug, emblazoned with the slogan 'SEXY BEAST', is right in her eye-line. Doctor Bradley must have been drinking from it just before she arrived, as she can smell a faint scent of coffee still clinging to it. She wonders whether it was a joke gift from someone else in the department, or a serious present from a former – or current – girlfriend, and realises just how little she knows about him.

'Thank you. That wasn't so hard, was it?'

'No, Doctor Bradley.' Her voice is small, little more than a squeak, and her punishment hasn't even begun yet. She's aware of him standing directly behind her and wants to turn her head, see what he's doing, but something compels her to stay where she is. She knows that, if she meets his gaze, she'll see a desire in it that matches her own. It's safer to think of him as detached, aloof, handing out this chastisement for the sake of correcting her behaviour, rather than acknowledge him as a man who lives to spank girls' bottoms.

Her skirt rode up when she bent over, and she knows

the seat of her panties is already on display. But Doctor Bradley wants more. He reaches for the hem and pulls it right up to her waist. Laura doesn't even attempt to stop him; the dress is so ridiculous, there's a part of her that would happily let him strip it off her.

When he turns his attention to her underwear, it's another matter entirely. Where the dress was an impediment, to be disposed of as quickly as possible, her panties are the prize, to be savoured before he inches them down. Laura tries not to whimper as he arranges them so they're bunched just below her crotch, leaving her arse bare and her pussy visible where it peeps from between her thighs. Her face burns with embarrassment – she really shouldn't be allowing him to take such liberties, yet she can't deny him anything.

'Very nice,' he observes. 'There's nothing better than a plump white bottom ready for its first spanking.'

She wants him to get on with it; now he's bared her, she wants the whole painful process to be over as soon as possible. Because it will be painful, there's no doubting that. Even before the gym shoe lands for the first time, she knows his aim is to reduce her to a sobbing, penitent mess. But she can't prepare herself adequately for the moment of impact, the heavy slap that stings as it thwacks against her unprotected flesh. Yelling in shock and anguish, Laura clutches at the desktop. She redoubles her screams as Doctor Bradley spanks her again and again, making sure to cover the whole surface of her arse.

Every fresh slap piles pain upon pain, the dull impact of one stroke barely fading away before another takes its place. She fights to retain some semblance of normality, of everything her tutorial sessions could be, focusing on the coffee mug so close to her face and repeating the words 'sexy beast' in her mind like a mantra to help her through this ordeal. That's what he is, she thinks, sexy and bestial, his cultured façade peeling away to reveal the horny, primal man below. A man who's taking pleasure in beating her backside till it's a throbbing, fiery ball of anguish.

Except somewhere in the process, the pain is joined by another sensation; endorphins kick in, bringing a sweet, secret pleasure with them. Laura still sobs, telling him she'll do anything he wants, anything, if he'll only stop spanking her, but her pussy is awash with juice and, as each blow drives her against the edge of the desk, she feels an answering jolt of sensation in her clit.

Lost in a world where pain and pleasure have become two faces of the same coin, it takes her a moment to realise she's got her wish. He's thrown down the plimsoll and her spanking is over. Instead of relief, she experiences only a strange sense of loss, but that's forgotten as Doctor Bradley's hand caresses her tortured cheeks. He gives a gruff chuckle of satisfaction, relishing the heat he's raised. His touch is soothing, and when he slips his hand lower, to slide his fingers through the wetness in her pussy, she pushes her bum back at him, wanting more.

'You're ready to be fucked, aren't you?' he comments, pushing first one, then a second finger into her pussy and meeting nothing in the way of resistance.

'Yes, Doctor Bradley.' She can't disguise the raw need in her voice.

His zip comes down, and he spends what seems to her an agonising amount of time fumbling and adjusting his clothing, but when he comes to her, pressing his body up close, she can feel his bare, hairy thighs against her skin. As his cock, sheathed in a condom, nudges between her pussy lips, seeking entrance, she realises she hasn't even seen it. But it's big, that much she knows as he penetrates her, pushing the walls of her cunt wide, and that suits her just fine. And excited as he must be by having spanked her, he's more than just a jackhammer. He takes his time about fucking her, pushing in as deep as he can go, his groin slapping against her arse with every stroke and reigniting the fire in her punished arse.

Laura clings on to the desk, buffeted by the force of his thrusts but welcoming his possession of her. How fortunes turn around, she thinks. Now she's begging him not to stop, and she doesn't care who else he might be seeing, or how he treats them, just as long as he fucks her to the edge of oblivion. His thrusts grow faster, more erratic, as he loses the fight to retain his self-control.

With a groan, he shoots his seed into the condom, holding her tight so she can feel every last pulse of his cock inside her. This is the crowning moment of everything he's done to her this afternoon, baring and spanking and fucking her, for her pleasure as well as his, and Laura surrenders to the orgasm that ripples through her core.

Almost regretfully, he pulls away from her, leaving her to pull up her panties and readjust her dress. Whether he throws her out of his tutorial group or not – and she still doesn't know whether that was just an idle threat, issued as part of the game – nothing will ever be quite the same between them.

Looking almost respectable once more, Doctor Bradley hunts through the papers they scattered as he screwed her on the desk, and eventually finds the one he wants. Her essay, the one he's just chewed her out over. Which, she sees as he hands it back, he's graded with a B minus. It's the best mark she's ever received from him.

He grins. 'I know I was harsh on you, but you've worked hard, Laura. And I'm hoping for better in your end-of-term paper. Though I may need to give you some extra tuition to help you through it ...'

She's still smiling as she shuts the door of his office behind her. She has the feeling that from now on her Wednesday afternoons are going to be devoted to Doctor Bradley, and to gaining the very best education a girl could want.

THE SILVER CHAIN – PRIMULA BOND

Good things come to those who wait…

After a chance meeting one evening, mysterious entrepreneur Gustav Levi and photographer Serena Folkes agree to a very special contract.

Gustav will launch Serena's photographic career at his gallery, but only if Serena agrees to become his companion.

To mark their agreement, Gustav gives Serena a bracelet and silver chain which binds them physically and symbolically. A sign that Serena is under Gustav's power.

As their passionate relationship intensifies, the silver chain pulls them closer together. But will Gustav's past tear them apart?

A passionate, unforgettable erotic romance for fans of *50 Shades of Grey* and Sylvia Day's *Crossfire Trilogy*.

GAME – JUSTINE ELYOT

The stakes are high, the game is on.

In this sequel to Justine Elyot's bestselling *On Demand*, Sophie discovers a whole new world of daring sexual exploits.

Sophie's sexual tastes have always been a bit on the wild side – something her boyfriend Lloyd has always loved about her.

But Sophie gives Lloyd every part of her body except her heart. To win all of her, Lloyd challenges Sophie to live out her secret fantasies.

As the game intensifies, she experiments with all kinds of kinks and fetishes in a bid to understand what she really wants. But Lloyd feature in her final decision? Or will the ultimate risk he takes drive her away from him?

Find out more at www.mischiefbooks.com

POWER PLAY – CHARLOTTE STEIN

Now she's the boss, everything that once seemed forbidden is possible…

Meet Eleanor Harding, a woman who loves to be in control and who puts Anastasia Steele in the shade.

When Eleanor is promoted, she loses two very important things: the heated relationship she had with her boss, and control over her own desires.

She finds herself suddenly craving something very different – and office junior, Ben, seems like just the sort of man to fulfil her needs. He's willing to show her all of the things she's been missing – namely, what it's like to be the one in charge.

Now all Eleanor has to do is decide…is Ben calling the kinky shots, or is she?

Find out more at www.mischiefbooks.com

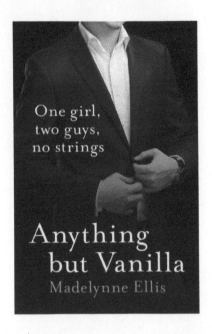

ANYTHING BUT VANILLA
MADELYNNE ELLIS

One girl, two guys, no strings.

Kara North is on the run. Fleeing from her controlling fiancé and a wedding she ne
wanted, she accepts the chance offer of refuge on Liddell Island, where she soor
catches the eye of the island's owner, erotic photographer Ric Liddell.

But pleasure comes in more than one flavour when Zachary Blackwater, the charm
ice-cream vendor also takes an interest, and wants more than just a tumble in the su

When Kara learns that the two men have been unlikely lovers for years, she becon
obsessed with the idea of a threesome.

Soon Kara is wondering how she ever considered committing herself to just one m

Find out more at www.mischiefbooks.com

www.ingramcontent.com/pod-product-compliance
Ingram Content Group UK Ltd.
Pitfield, Milton Keynes, MK11 3LW, UK
UKHW022245180325
456436UK00001B/21

9 780007 534838